Lawfully Ours

Brides of Cedar Falls, Book #9

Jo Grafford, writing as Jovie Grace

JG Press

SECOND EDITION April 2025: This book was originally part of the Lawkeepers Series. It has since been rewritten and expanded to be part the **Brides of Cedar Falls Series** — swoony historical romance full of faith, hope, love, and cowboys!

ISBN: 978-1-63907-085-5

Acknowledgments

A huge, heartfelt thank you to my editor, Cathleen Weaver, for working her magic on this story, along with Karen Edwards. I'm also enormously grateful to my beta reader, Mahasani. Another big shout-out goes to all the Cuppa Jo Readers out there for reading and loving my books!

For more about my books —>

Follow on Bookbub
https://www.bookbub.com/authors/jovie-grace

Follow on Amazon
https://www.amazon.com/author/joviegrace

Read FREE Bonus Stories
https://www.JoGrafford.com/bonuscontent

Join Cuppa Jo Readers
https://www.facebook.com/groups/CuppaJoReaders

Chapter 1: Close Calls
Jack

June, 1873

A rumble of thunder made Jack Holiday's horse nicker in complaint. He was on the final stretch of his hundred-mile journey to Cedar Falls, hoping to beat the rain. It wasn't safe to be riding alone through the unsettled Texas rangeland. It was infested with rattlesnakes. Even worse, it was crawling with outlaws who wouldn't hesitate to take out a grudge on a federal marshal.

Jack understood the risks, but he was determined to beat the odds, since his new assignment was time sensitive. Every hour he spent on the road was one less hour he'd have to track the notorious outlaw who'd been spotted in the area.

Billy Bob Flint.

The son of a Comanche war chief and a pioneer woman, Flint had spent the last several years making a name for himself as a modern-day Robin Hood. Not only had his cattle and horse thieving spree cost the local ranchers dearly, Jack's superiors were even more afraid of what he might be planning. Unfortunately, they had no hard evidence to support any of their running theories. There'd been no reports of selling re-branded livestock and no bank accounts identified in Flint's name. There'd been no trail of money whatsoever. It was as if the cattle and horses he'd rustled had disappeared into thin air.

Despite the lack of any evidence to go on, what the government feared most was an uprising. There were pockets of displaced Comanches embedded throughout the foothills, whole families of them who continued to resist being relocated to government-sanctioned reservations. For this reason, they wanted Billy Bob Flint brought in for questioning as soon as possible.

Though Jack sympathized with the plight of the Comanches, he wasn't paid to have an opinion on the matter. He was paid to follow orders and round up criminals. Nothing more. Nothing less. Only time would tell if Billy Bob Flint was the criminal his accusers claimed him to be.

Another crack of thunder sounded. It was closer this time. Jack could feel aftershocks all the way to his bones. Every instinct in him was telling him there was a storm brewing in this part of the country that had little to do with the rainclouds festering overhead.

That was why one federal marshal in particular was being sent to put an end to it. A lawman who always got his man.

Me.

The first fat drops of rain pelted down on Jack's head and shoulders, dampening his vest and shirt. He pulled the brim of his Stetson lower over his eyes as he and his horse pushed through the steadily rising wind. The natural elements weren't sparing them any punches this afternoon.

"Come on, Larkspur," he urged. "Almost there."

She nickered again and increased her stride.

Hating the necessity of riding her for so many miles straight, Jack leaned forward in his saddle, trying not to think about how wet and chilly he was becoming. The breeze that was blowing in the rainclouds was quickly chasing away the summer warmth.

He patted the horse's neck, pleased with the young mare he'd been given at the last outpost. According to the Texas Ranger who'd saddled her for him, she'd been given her name because of the splash of white between her eyes. Not only was it in stark contrast to her otherwise brown coat, the splash of whiteness resembled the petals of a larkspur. Though some marshals traded their mounts for a fresh one at every stop, he was in no hurry to part with this one.

The rain waxed and waned for the next few miles. So did the feeling that he was being watched. The familiar prickle of awareness crept between Jack's shoulder blades and made its way down his spine.

He scanned the distant mountains, but all he saw were a few scruffy bushes and buffalo grass blowing in the breeze — no glowing eyes of a wild animal, nor the glint of a rifle barrel. He was traveling west along the Red River. The town of Cedar Falls would appear on the horizon at any second.

Yes, indeed. Any second now would be appreciated.

The rain abruptly ceased and was replaced by a sultry stillness. It blanketed Jack and his horse with a heavy, menacing feeling — like the brief calm before the rainstorm began again in earnest.

"Lord God, help us reach Cedar Falls before..." He ended his prayer right there, not wanting to voice any of the calamities that could still befall him during the final minutes of his trip.

A piercing scream made his head swivel toward the sound. It had the eerie, inhuman quality of a wildcat, but Jack knew better. According to his research, the displaced Comanche warriors were all too skilled at fading into their environment — right down to mimicking the calls of wild animals. They were especially fond of recreating the sounds of creatures who instilled the most fear in their listeners.

Another scream made his head swivel the other way. It was followed by a rumble of hooves from multiple directions, telling him he was surrounded on three sides. More hooves thundered his way, gaining momentum.

He stole a glance over his shoulder, and his blood chilled at the dust clouds rising behind him. He knew of only one thing that could turn semi-damp terrain into seething, churning clods of dirt like that. Somehow, he'd managed to ride into the path of a stampede. Either that, or someone was purposely driving a herd of creatures in his direction. From the occasional screams that met his ears, he was betting the latter was the case.

He frantically scanned the terrain in front of him, and his gaze landed on a bulbous outcropping of stone. It lay about a quarter mile ahead of him and Larkspur. As he drew closer, he could make out an overhang on one side that looked like it continued around to the front.

He dug his heels into Larkspur's trembling sides, urging her toward the rocky haven as the sound of hooves drew ever closer.

Jack tugged on the reins as they neared the stony outcropping, but Larkspur refused to slow her speed.

"Whoa, girl! Whoa!" He bellowed the words, pulling

harder on the reins. Now wasn't the time to give the horse her head. She was too terrified.

She finally slowed down enough for him to leap from the saddle. He jogged alongside her for a moment, keeping a firm hold on the reins. She overran the outcropping, finally halting a few strides in front of it.

Her eyes rolled back in her head, showing the whites of them. She tried to rear back on her hind legs, but he held her down with every ounce of strength in him.

"Easy, Larkspur. Easy." He leaped directly in front of her to meet her wide-eyed, glazed-over stare. By sheer willpower, he backed her toward the outcropping of rock until her rump grazed it. He propelled her down to the ground, first to her haunches and then to a lying position. The entire time, he kept up a steady crooning of words meant to reassure her. It was an impossible task, considering how violently his own heart was pounding. However, there was nowhere else for them to go. They couldn't possibly outrun whoever or whatever was heading their way.

He dropped to a crouch, craning around the side of their rocky refuge to gauge the progress of their pursuers.

What he saw wasn't quite what he'd been expecting from the sound of things.

Instead of a herd of buffalo, an army of Longhorns were headed their way — hundreds of them in a riot of colors. There were dappled browns, solid white bulls, and dusty black ones. They were traveling so closely together that some of them were goring each other with the pointy tips of their horns, eliciting trumpets of pain and alarm.

A Comanche rider rode bareback on his horse down one side of the herd, driving them forward with his short, piercing shrieks. The Longhorns increased their pace, bellowing all the louder in alarm.

Jack drew back inside his rocky haven, leaning over Larkspur and using his broad shoulders to block her view of what was happening. In a burst of inspiration, he loosened the buttons of his vest and wrapped the fabric around her ears. It was nothing short of a miracle that she hadn't lunged back to her feet and given away their hiding place.

"God, be with us," he muttered. "All of our hope is in You." It was where his hope had been for the past ten years as a lawman. The good Lord was the only One who hadn't let him down.

Though his situation was precarious at best, there was a part of him that was relieved to discover he and Larkspur had inadvertently gotten caught in the path of a few frontiersmen herding cattle. It was a whole lot better than being the target of a purposely induced stampede, none of which reduced the danger he and Larkspur were in at the moment. All it would take was one wrong move on his or his horse's part to get them trampled to death.

Placing his hands over Larkspur's ears, he silently prayed an age-old Biblical passage. There was nothing else he could do.

The Lord is my shepherd; I shall not want. He maketh me to lie down in green pastures. (Or dusty foothills, in their case.) *He leadeth me beside the still waters. He restoreth my soul; He leadeth me in the paths of righteousness for His name's sake.*

Unfortunately, those paths had taken an unexpectedly horrific turn.

The Longhorns rumbled abreast of his hiding place, pouring around both sides of the rocky outcropping, mooing loud enough to disturb the dead. Jack pressed his hands more firmly over the ears of his trembling horse and continued the prayer inside his head.

Yea, though I walk through the valley of the shadow of death, I will fear no evil; for Thou art with me.

At least he hoped that was the case.

The thundering herd kicked up so much dust, he was forced to close his eyes and press his face to the top of Larkspur's head.

She shuddered beneath his hands, emitting terrified whinnies. To his relief, she still made no attempt to stand, which was a good thing. If she'd truly had her heart set on bolting, he wouldn't have been able to stop her.

The Longhorns thundering by on either side of them were kicking up so much dust and dirt that Jack could taste the grit of them in his mouth. He kept his forehead pressed to the top of Larkspur's head, willing her to keep holding still. The next few minutes proved to be the longest in his life. Each time the Comanche riders screamed, he could feel the answering jolt work its way through the horse.

Then it was over.

The last of the herd trotted past, right down to the stragglers. The screams of the riders and the sounds of mooing grew fainter.

Jack cracked his eyelids open and discovered he and Larkspur were coated in sandy dirt. Rocking back on his heels, he removed his hat and clapped it against his thigh, creating a whole new cloud of dust.

The sound of a gun being cocked alerted him to the fact that he and Larkspur were not alone.

"Lay your guns on the ground, cowboy. Both of them."

The drawling male voice caught Jack by surprise. It

sounded nothing like the wild screams of the other Comanche herdsmen, though there was still something in the man's accent that hinted at his Comanche bloodline.

"Pronto. I haven't got all day." The voice was laced with impatience and an unexpected edge of humor. "Put 'em on the ground and kick 'em in my direction."

Knowing he was a dead man anyway, Jack didn't see any choice but to comply. If he attempted to draw his weapons, he'd be shot before he could finish locating the owner of the voice. There was still so much dirt and dust caking his eyelashes that he didn't dare open his eyes all the way.

"Now toss me a change of clothing from your saddlebag."

What? It was an odd request. Most robbers demanded money, which Jack happened to be traveling with plenty of. However, the request to empty his pockets never came.

The man took the clothing Jack handed over. Then he tossed a coil of rope over Jack's shoulder. It slid to the dirt in front of him.

"Last request. Tie your feet together."

Last request. The words had an ominous ring to them. Nausea churned in Jack's belly as he picked up the rope, wondering why the fellow didn't simply put a bullet between his eyes and get it over with. Was he in the mood to inflict the maximum amount of pain on Jack first? Was he about to be tied to the back of his horse and dragged across the rangeland until there was nothing left than a few strands of skin and fabric hanging to his bones?

"*Rápido!* Hurry, *hombre!*"

Despite the bandit's use of a few Spanish words, he didn't have a Spanish accent. He didn't possess the heavy, guttural accent of a full-blooded Indian, either.

Who are you?

Jack longed to shake his head like a mangy dog to dislodge the layer of dust coating his face. That way, he could turn around and look his fill of the man who would soon punch his ticket and send him to Kingdom Come.

"There's a town due west of here on the other side of the river," the drawling voice continued. "No more'n five miles. After I leave, you'd best make your way there before nightfall. It's not safe for you out here alone. There's a tailor by the name of Cat Southerland who might be willing to replace the clothing I took off your hands. For a fee, of course. One I couldn't afford."

Jack was so astounded to discover the man didn't intend to kill him that his hands faltered on the knot he was tying around his ankles. It wasn't because he was afraid. At the seasoned age of thirty-two, he very much understood the dangers he assumed every time he pinned on his badge. He simply couldn't fathom why any outlaw would choose to spare his life.

On second thought, he could think of one bandit who rarely did what was expected. One bandit alone who'd managed to baffle every lawman within a several-hundred-mile radius.

Jack finished tying his legs together and pivoted on his knees to face his captor. He kept his hands raised in submission.

Though he hadn't asked for permission to turn around, he instinctively knew the man wasn't going to shoot him. He knew this for a fact because he'd done his research. He'd spent the last two months interviewing anyone who'd ever so much as caught a glimpse of the man. He'd spoken with Texas Rangers, farmers, ranchers, and sheriffs. He'd even visited a handful of outlaws awaiting trial, outlaws who'd supposedly had a run-in with the very man he was looking for.

The man he was now facing.

Billy Bob Flint.

Jack shook the dust from his head and blew a few puffs of air to clear his vision. Then all he could do was stare. From the number of sketches he'd viewed on various Wanted posters, he'd been expecting the notorious outlaw to look more savage. More wild-eyed. More heathen. He'd half-expected to find a quiver of arrows slung across his shoulder.

What he hadn't pictured was the man staring at him now from the back of his horse. Though Billy Bob Flint was in sore need of a haircut, his brown hair wasn't long enough to be braided like the Indians. It waved against his neck in sweaty tendrils beneath a slouched Stetson. His shirt and trousers were a sun-bleached gray that had seen better days beneath a curious array of patches. All in all, his clothing wasn't much different from what any other male settler might be wearing.

His features were more tanned than swarthy, and he wasn't brandishing any weapons. There were no hatchets or knives in sight, no bows or rifles slung across his shoulder or the rump of his horse which he was riding bareback.

"Should I impress on you the many reasons why you shouldn't attempt to follow me, *hombre?*" Flint's black gaze glittered over Jack and Larkspur, feeling like it missed nothing. It rested for a moment on the dusty star pinned to Jack's vest, then rose a few inches higher to his face.

Jack's heart sank, wondering if he was a dead man now that the outlaw understood exactly what he was dealing with. "Every man with a badge is hunting you." It wasn't a threat. It was a statement of fact, a reminder that executing him in cold blood would only increase the number of crosshairs on the outlaw's forehead.

"I am aware." Billy Bob's jaw hardened. "All for the crime of taking back what's rightfully mine."

Jack frowned as he repeated the man's words inside his head. He could only presume he was referring to the plight of his people. He was also struck by the fact that Billy Bob Flint spoke such excellent English. There was no record of him being educated in any school. He probably had his mother to thank for his learning.

He held Billy Bob's gaze. "I reckon you're referring to the Longhorns that passed by us a few minutes ago?"

"I am. Contrary to what you've likely heard about me, I only round up the wild ones. I've never laid a finger on a single animal bearing a brand on his rump."

Jack's eyebrows rose. That was news to him, though he was unsure why the outlaw was bothering to plead his case to a dusty marshal on his knees. Jack was neither a judge nor a jury. Though he was carrying the warrant for Billy Bob's arrest, he wasn't the one who would ultimately decide the man's fate.

"You're right. I was told a very different story about you." He saw no point in mincing words with someone who was being so brutally honest with him. "But I prefer to do my own thinking and form my own opinions." None of which had proven easy since the day he'd crossed the border between Oklahoma and Texas. Here in the rangeland, the lines were all too often blurred between good and evil, between the right side of the law and the wrong side of it. So much so that it occasionally challenged the very reason he'd chosen his line of work — to get justice for those who needed it the most.

Today was one of those days. Just listening to Billy Bob

Flint talk was enough to blur the lines on the many files Jack had read about the man. What if the information in them hadn't been entirely true? Was it possible he was being framed for crimes he hadn't committed? If so, who was behind the allegations and what did they hope to gain from them?

"If you've got something on your mind, Marshal...?" Flint's upper lip curled in the faintest of smiles that didn't reach his eyes.

"It's nothing I care to share at the moment, other than this. I *will* continue to do my own thinking, and I *will* continue to form my own opinions." It was the best answer he could offer at the moment. He was banking on the odds that Billy Bob Flint preferred hearing the truth over meaningless platitudes and empty assurances.

"In that case," the outlaw gave a satisfied grunt, half-turning his horse around, "you'd best find a room to rent, because you're going to be in town for a while."

Jack tasted disappointment. After coming face-to-face with the man he was tracking, he hated being forced to watch him ride away. There was nothing he could do to stop him, though.

"They sent me to find you," he offered quietly. It was foolish to admit such a thing, but it might be his only chance to question the fellow in a non-formal setting. He watched him closely for his reaction.

"Figured that." Billy Bob spat the words from the side of his mouth. "It's not the first time the government sent someone after me, and it probably won't be the last."

Unless I arrest you, Jack corrected inside his head. "It means we'll be seeing each other again after you ride away," he taunted. *Assuming you don't shoot me before you go.* Again, it was probably foolish to point out that the outlaw could easily prevent Jack from following him — permanently. But Jack preferred doing things his way. And right now, extending the outlaw a little trust felt like the right strategy to employ.

This was the moment in which his current theory about Billy Bob Flint would stand on its own merit or die a quick and ugly death. It was the moment Billy Bob Flint's true character would manifest itself.

Flint's expression didn't change. "Perhaps." He patted his horse's neck in a surprisingly affectionate move. "And perhaps not." He leaned forward. "Hyaaaa!" He pressed his knees into his horse's sides, urging the creature after the fast-retreating herd of Longhorns.

Jack stared after him, more convinced than ever that there was more to Billy Bob Flint's story than what he'd been told. It took him less than a minute to untie himself and stand. He could've leaped into the saddle to ride after the outlaw, but something told him the answers he was seeking wouldn't be found in the fast-falling shadows. Not this evening, at any rate.

His gut told him that the answers he was seeking awaited him in Cedar Falls. Not only was it the closest town, it was the same place Flint himself had encouraged him to spend the night. More specifically, he'd dropped the name of a tailor, a woman by the name of Cat Southerland.

There had to be a reason for it.

There also had to be a reason why his guns remained on the ground where he'd kicked them. The fact that Billy Bob had left them behind didn't feel like an accident. Jack hurriedly jogged over to them to scoop them up and shove them back in his holsters.

No sooner did he slide into the saddle than the skies

opened up. In seconds, he was soaked to the skin, and he no longer had any dry clothing to change into upon his arrival.

The breeze picked up, chilling Jack further as the skyline of Cedar Falls drew into view. Through the sheeting rain, he could see the outline of rustic storefront buildings. Men and women were hurrying down the sidewalks on both sides of the road with their heads bent against the wind and rain. Many of them had umbrellas spread open.

Jack kept his eyes peeled for any sign of an inn or another business with a room for rent.

And there it was.

Cedar Falls Inn.

The name of it was engraved on a sign that was swinging wildly in the wind. The two-story structure boasted weathered wooden siding and a front veranda with a hodgepodge of rockers and chairs. Sandstone urns brimmed with desert roses on either side of the door.

He was so busy salivating over the hot meal the inn would be serving for dinner that the woman stepping off the sidewalk into his path caught him by surprise. Larkspur reared back on her hind legs, scissoring her front hooves in the air with a shriek of warning.

The woman dropped to all fours on the rain-slick cobblestones lining the edge of the street. The packages she'd been carrying went tumbling from her grasp.

Jack pressed his knees hard to Larkspur's flanks to avoid being unseated, pulling on the reins in an attempt to turn the horse in mid-air to prevent her hooves from crashing down on the hapless woman. He could only pray she hadn't already been kicked.

As soon as he returned Larkspur to all fours, he leaped out of the saddle and crouched down beside the woman. Her brown calico gown was soaked with rain and spattered with mud. The parcels she'd been carrying were equally muddy.

"Are you alright, ma'am?" His hands came down on her shoulders, preparing to lift her to her feet.

"Yes. I thank you." Her voice came out harried and nervous, but her features weren't contorted with pain, and no sounds of weeping ensued.

He tried to take comfort in that. "I'm sorry about nearly trampling you with my horse. Truly sorry, ma'am."

She was still for a moment. Then she twisted his way, revealing a dark-eyed beauty behind the sodden hood pulled up over her hair. Hair the color of rich coffee grounds. There was something vaguely familiar about her high cheekbones and the proud slant of her forehead, though he wasn't sure what it was.

At the moment, he couldn't think clearly at all. The way she was looking at him held him riveted — with anxious scrutiny and a curious brand of wistfulness. Never before had he been so drawn to someone. It was especially puzzling, considering that they'd just met. He didn't even know her name.

Yet.

"It's alright," she said softly. "I'm the one who was distracted and not watching where I was going, Mr. ah—" She grew abruptly silent as her gaze landed on his badge. Despite the deepening twilight, there was no mistaking the way her face paled.

"Jack Holiday," he supplied smoothly as he helped her to her feet. He was accustomed to people getting all twitchy after finding out he was a lawman. Granted, those who got the twitchiest often had the most to hide.

"I'm Cat Southerland," she returned, looking so discomfited that he was fearful all over again that she might be injured.

"Unbelievable," he muttered. "Would you believe it if I told you you're exactly the woman I was hoping to find?" What were the odds of crossing paths with her so soon after Billy Bob Flint had uttered her name?

"Me?" She swayed on her feet, looking alarmingly close to passing out. "You've been looking for me?"

His hands shot out to grasp her elbows. "My apologies for upsetting you, ma'am." He hastened to explain. "It's just that I find myself in need of a tailor, and your services come highly recommended by a traveler I met on the road." It didn't feel prudent to identify the outlaw who'd sung her praises or the way he'd bemoaned her prices.

She grimaced. "I'm actually a weaver, so I'm not sure why anyone would recommend my sewing. Who was this traveler?"

"I didn't catch his name." It wasn't an outright lie, since Billy Bob Flint hadn't precisely introduced himself. It hadn't been necessary. "If you don't wish to be troubled by my order, perhaps you could recommend a different tailor. I already have my measurements." But he begged her with his eyes to reconsider. Despite the rain, he found himself oddly reluctant to bring their encounter to a close.

"Oh, it's no trouble," she assured quickly, "as long as you don't require something too elaborate. I can weave fabric fit for royalty, but my sewing skills run along simpler lines."

"I don't need anything fancy," he assured. "With the amount of time I spend in the saddle, I value durability above all else."

"That I can do." She beamed at him through the raindrops. It was a smile that lit her entire face. "Since it's Friday, I can get started right away."

Jack wasn't sure what Friday had to do with it, but he nodded. He was only half listening. The rest of his thoughts were focused on figuring out Billy Bob Flint's interest in Miss Southerland. There was nothing about her demure calico gown that would suggest she was engaged in a life of crime on the side.

"On weekdays, I serve as the companion of a woman named Winifred Monroe," she babbled as she collected the packages she'd dropped. "She owns the rail yard."

He helped her gather her packages, clumsily bumping fingers as he handed them to her. Neither of them were wearing gloves. Despite the damp breeze blowing, her fingers were warm to the touch. For the briefest of moments, he longed to lean into that warmth, but his better judgment took over. He wasn't yet sure what Cat Southerland's ties were to Billy Bob Flint, so he would need to proceed with caution until he figured it out.

She glanced furtively down the street in the direction he'd ridden in from before confiding in a soft voice, "It's a new position that I stumbled across by accident, but I'm so glad that I did. I've truly enjoyed living in Cedar Falls."

The wistful note in her voice made no sense to him, though it stirred his sympathy. It sounded like she was uncertain how long she would remain in town.

For a man who rarely stayed in one place for long, it shouldn't have bothered him as much as it did.

Chapter 2: Cedar Falls
Cat

Saturday evening

C at's eyes took on a dry and burning sensation, reminding her how long she'd been at her loom. More than twelve hours, not counting a brief lunch break. She pushed back her chair and lifted the watch pendent dangling on the necklace at her throat and discovered it was quarter 'til seven.

Whew! It was past the dinner hour. All too often lately, she'd been keeping her looms spinning far into the evening to fill the ever-increasing demand for her custom fabric designs. This was one of those evenings.

Fortunately, one of her coworkers at the Bent Horseshoe Ranch had offered to help today. Molly was new to the art of weaving, but she was turning out to be a quick learner. It helped that she was already a skilled seamstress. Her offer of assistance had come in the nick of time. Not in Cat's wildest imagination had she pictured turning her newly purchased looms into such a thriving business so quickly.

She'd been born not too far from Cedar Falls and had chosen to move back a few months ago. After being gone nearly a decade from the remote cattle town, she was banking on no one recognizing the adult version of her. During the time she'd been gone, countless more farms and ranches had been built — too many to count. It was still a relatively small community, but it was booming with commerce.

To top it all off, Cat owned the only two looms within a comfortable riding distance, giving her an easy monopoly on the local fabric market. The only folks she knew who were still ordering fabric from out of town were the uppity seam-stresses employed by the Cedar Falls Finishing School for Young Ladies. They imported Italian silk and such for their ballgowns. *Oh, la la!*

She smothered a yawn as she scooted her stool back from her loom. For the life of her, she couldn't fathom why anyone would even need a ballgown in a town this small, much less a finishing school. However, the headmistress of the school, Rachel Cassidy, ordered enough yards of calico, linen, and wool from her that it was difficult to take offense to the school's other hoity-toity purchasing habits.

Molly pushed back her stool, too. "My brother will arrive at any second to take me home." Jed Price was the proud owner of a herd of sheep on the small cotton farm he'd inherited from the grandparents who'd raised them. Their claim to the deed was dubious at best, but Cat's brother had sworn her to secrecy about how the Price family had actually gotten their hands on it. The only thing that mattered now was that Cat had managed to negotiate a weekly supply of wool and cotton from Jed upon her arrival in town.

Molly stretched her back and brushed a few threads off

her ruffled white apron. During the week, she served as Winifred Monroe's personal maid at the massive Bent Horseshoe Ranch. Most of her weekends were spent at her brother's farm, but Jed had encouraged her to accept Cat's offer to hire her for the day — probably because they could use the extra cash.

"Of course. Go." Cat murmured, reaching for the pouch she kept her small savings in. She carefully counted out a few coins and held them out to Molly. Her friend would be spending the night at her brother's home and attending church with him in the morning.

"Thank you." As Molly gratefully pocketed the money, her gaze fell on the sign Cat had stayed up late last night to paint. "What a lovely sign! The paint is the same shade as the bluebells that grow wild all over town." It read *Souther-land Sewing* in pale blue letters on a weathered strip of wood. Someday, the sign would hang in the window of Cat's own shop. For now, though, she was taking advantage of their mutual employer's generosity.

"I'm glad you like it. Now all I need is a shop to go with it." Cat's voice was wry. *Assuming I get to stay in town long enough to live out that particular dream.* Her encounter with the federal marshal yesterday had kept her up last night. It was yet unclear if his presence in town was something she needed to worry about. She'd gone to a lot of trouble to distance herself from any connection to her outlaw brother, even changing her name. If anyone guessed the truth about her, she'd probably find herself on the run again.

More's the pity.

She was currently serving as Winifred Monroe's companion during the week, while the aging woman's niece and nephews kept her company over the weekend. It was a job she almost felt guilty accepting money for, since she benefitted the most from their arrangement. Not only did Ms. Monroe generously provide her with room and board, she always insisted on Cat joining the rest of her staff in the kitchen for meals.

Free food. Her stomach growled at the thought of another slice of the cook's sourdough bread. Cat's mouth watered in anticipation of slathering it with the strawberry preserves made from Ms. Monroe's own berry patch.

"You'll get your shop. I know you will." Molly gazed around the vast attic room that doubled as Cat's bedroom and workspace. "This is just a stepping stone, my friend. You're going places. I felt it in my bones the moment we met."

You have no idea. It was a deadly accurate statement, considering how long Cat had been on the run. She'd gone places alright. Too many places. She was weary of moving so often and longed to remain in Cedar Falls — never to leave again.

Not while living indefinitely in Ms. Monroe's attic, of course, but in a storefront building of her own. Maybe one with a loft apartment that would allow her to live on site.

In the meantime, Ms. Winifred had allowed her to move her few belongings to a finished-off area of the attic. It was bigger than any of her regular guest rooms, and it contained a useful collection of work tables. It also contained a rustic desk where Cat's sewing machine rested.

Every item of furniture in the space had been pilfered from the odds and ends that populated the rest of Ms. Monroe's attic. A wall of mix-and-match shelves displayed Cat's rolls of fabric. During the past week, the mercantile owners downtown had purchased nearly as many yards from her inventory as the owners of the finishing school.

A wide, curtained screen separated her workspace from her bed and the silver tub where she bathed. It was a humble setup with no frills, but it wasn't costing her a penny. Even more importantly, it allowed her to keep the low profile she so desperately needed as the only remaining family member of a notorious outlaw. At least, that's what most folks called her brother. It wasn't true, of course, but he'd yet to find a lawman willing to listen to his plea of innocence.

"I appreciate your vote of confidence." Cat infused as much warmth into her voice as she could. If and when she was ever forced to depart Cedar Falls, she would hate leaving Molly behind most of all. They'd grown close during the short time they'd known each other.

"I think I'm going to stay up a little longer to finish sewing Mr. Holiday's new shirt." Though Cat spoke as casually as she could, her heart gave a crazy little flutter at the memory of her first encounter with the tall, darkly tanned, and ruggedly handsome marshal.

Her brother had instructed her to keep her head down and avoid lawmen. All of them. He'd claimed that many of them were sellouts — more interested in making a name for themselves than administering true justice. He'd also warned her that a growing number of them were secretly on the payrolls of some of the worst scoundrels west of the Mississippi River.

Though Cat couldn't picture the overly serious, by-the-books Mr. Holiday compromising his integrity, not for any amount of dirty money, she didn't know that for sure. After only one encounter with him, she couldn't claim to know him at all.

But I want to.

She swallowed a sigh. As for ignoring the man like her

brother had advised, well, that hadn't been so easy after accidentally stepping into the path of his horse. A less skilled rider would've trampled her to death, but Mr. Holiday's horsemanship had proven to be faultless. By the time she'd realized he was a federal marshal, they were already conversing.

And I was already drowning in his piercing brown eyes.

"I look forward to meeting this Mr. Holiday." Molly's sly voice yanked Cat from her impossible daydream.

Cat blinked at her. "Why is that?"

Molly smoothed a hand over her hair, tucking a stray strand behind one ear. "Because this is the first time any man in this town has given my favorite weaver the faraway look she's wearing now."

"Nonsense!" Cat sniffed. "I think you're mistaking my tiredness for something it's not."

"Prove it." Molly playfully lifted her chin.

"How?" Cat knew better than anyone else that her daydreams about the handsome Jack Holiday were going nowhere.

"By joining my brother and I for dinner at the Cedar Falls Inn." Molly folded her arms in challenge.

Cat was surprised to discover they were eating out instead of eating at home. Normally, her friends were more frugal with their finances than that. "How will that prove anything?"

Molly gave her a triumphant look. "Because Mr. Holiday happens to be staying at the inn, so the probability he will dine there this evening is high."

A helpless chuckle escaped Cat. "Are you suggesting I pursue a federal marshal who's likely in the middle of tracking down a dangerous criminal?" Considering what her brother did for a living, it felt most unwise to go out of her way to draw the man's attention to herself.

"Quite the opposite!" Molly unfolded her arms, treating her to a look of mock indignation. "I'm asking you to prove your indifference to the man by sailing right past him with your nose in the air." A merry chuckle pealed out of her. "And keep me company while my oh-so-smitten brother wastes his time wooing a woman who will never return the sentiment."

Ah. "So, *that's* why you're dining out this evening." It made sense now. Cat recalled Molly grumbling earlier about some woman who'd caught Jed's eyes, but she'd only been half listening. She was too new in town to know many people.

"That is exactly why we're dining out." Her friend's expression grew pleading. "And since you're my dearest friend in the world, you're going to have pity on me and say yes."

Though Cat typically saved every penny she could, she'd already worked through the dinner hour at the Monroe household. She'd been planning to pilfer something simple from the kitchen before heading to bed. Something that didn't require any cooking.

"It's a tempting offer for sure." She stood and carried her dying candle to the washbasin. Something sharp pierced her toe, bringing her to a halt. "Ouch!" She bent to retrieve a pin poking through the toe of her slipper. She must have dropped it earlier while pinning the sleeves to Jack Holiday's shirt.

Tapping her toe to stop the stinging, she leaned closer to the mirror hanging over the washbasin to inspect her hair. *Not too bad after a full day's work.* Her long dark hair was pulled up in the back, with thick glossy curls dangling around her temples and cheeks. Her creamy calico skirt was a bit wrinkled, but the small red flowers and green stems she'd woven into the fabric drew the viewer's eye away from the wrinkles.

"Oh, for pity's sake! You're a China doll with dimples, more than presentable enough to make an appearance in the dining room at Cedar Falls Inn." Molly moved toward the door, tweaking her grass green muslin skirts over her more ample curves. Her auburn hair was coiled high, and her striking blue eyes were glittering with impatience. "Never fear. Your skulking, overprotective brother high-tailed it out of town yesterday, so he'll be none the wiser about your dinner plans."

Cat rolled her eyes in the mirror at her friend. "Over-protective is putting it mildly. He all but forbade me to court anyone. Ever." If he had it his way, she would grow into a ripe old spinster like her employer.

Molly grimaced. "I prefer your brother's skulking to my brother's snapping and snarling at every eligible gentleman who dares look my way." Though she was very much aware of Cat's brother ducking in and out of the shadows to pay unscheduled visits, she never asked questions about him. Not so much as his name. She seemed to understand that his infrequent appearances were something Cat wasn't at liberty to discuss.

"We make quite a pair, don't we?" Cat carried her candle over to the nightstand beside her bed, where she set it down and blew it out. "The town's untouchables." Both of them were well into their marriageable years at the age of twenty-four. Little good it did them, though, with the rabid watchdog brothers they possessed.

"Is that a yes to my dinner invitation?" Molly eagerly ushered Cat toward the door with both hands.

"You know it is," Cat grumbled, trudging her way.

"Good." Molly sounded gleeful. "At least we'll have each other to grow old with. That's something, right?"

It was more than something. Cat gratefully looped her arm through Molly's arm, and together they glided down the two sets of stairs leading to the main level.

Rupert, Ms. Monroe's stately butler and right-hand man, was waiting for them by the front door. "Your brother is waiting for you in his wagon, Miss Price." He was a dignified man of middling years who was rarely seen in anything other than the black suit that served as his uniform.

"I've been invited to go to dinner with them." Cat gave him a sunny smile, suddenly glad for an excuse to leave her looms and sewing machine behind for a few hours. The cramped muscles in her neck and shoulders were more than ready for a break.

"Indeed?" Though Rupert rarely showed much expression, the somber lines of his features twisted in surprise.

"Yes. If you'll please inform Ms. Monroe of my whereabouts, I'd be most appreciative."

He frowned in concern. "Will you be needing a ride back from the farm, Miss Southerland?"

"Not at all," Molly cut in happily. "Jed won't mind bringing her back, and the farm isn't where we're heading, anyway. My brother has it in his stubborn head to woo a certain new waitress at the Cedar Falls Inn." She made a face at Rupert. "I know it isn't kind to talk about folks behind their backs, but it doesn't break my heart one bit to see Bea Hazelwood eating a little humble pie."

If anything, the somber lines around Rupert's mouth grew even more pronounced. "Losing one's fortune overnight can't have been easy on her or her family. I imagine she could use a friend right now." He inclined his head in gentle admonishment at her and Cat.

Molly snorted. "She already has plenty of friends, and I can guarantee she wouldn't welcome your pity or mine."

"You may be right." He inclined his head at them again. "Enjoy your dinner at the inn, ladies."

"That we will. Thank you." Molly tugged Cat out the door without any further ado.

Jed was not only waiting for them beside his wagon, he was wearing his second-best suit, and his sandy-blonde hair was still damp from a bath.

Molly teased him mercilessly about it all the way to the downtown area, enough to make his face red beneath his freckles.

Cat felt sorry for him. He was a hardworking farmer, honest to a fault, and painfully shy. Though he was a few years older than her, he'd not once made any attempt to court her, for which she was grateful. Because of her close friendship with Molly, she'd always viewed him as more like a brother than a potential suitor.

The dusty trail transitioned into the hard-packed dirt road of Main Street. It was lined with storefront buildings on both sides. Many of them stood two stories tall, while others bore false second-story fronts.

The weathered wooden walls of Cedar Falls Inn drew into view. Though the sun was setting, the street lanterns cast a warm glow across the front porch of the inn, illuminating a line of urns brimming with summer roses.

Cat's gaze drifted down the street to the tall, white-steepled church. Every time she laid eyes on the building, it served as a reminder that God was always watching. It was a view she found comfort in. It was also a view that never failed to stir her guilt.

She blew out a silent breath, struggling to tamp down on the discontentment surging through her. Only because of the many sacrifices her younger brother had made for her had she been able to afford the pair of looms sitting in her attic bedroom. Since he was the one who'd suggested she move back to Cedar Falls, she could indirectly thank him for the roof over her head, too.

After being forced to go on the run together, he'd made sure she had a place to stay and plenty to eat. Lately, though, she'd found herself longing for more — more education, more elevated connections, more friends, more money, more of all the things their life on the run had stripped them of; and Billy Bob had seen fit to give them to her. He'd said it was only right for her to move on with her life since her face wasn't the one on the Wanted posters. However, that didn't keep her from feeling guilty about putting down roots again while he continued to be on the run.

Molly nudged her with her shoulder. "A penny for your thoughts."

Cat smiled and reached for her reticule, but Molly swatted her hand away. "I wasn't asking for a real penny, and you know it. Let me guess." She lowered her voice so Jed couldn't hear what she said next. "You were daydreaming about a certain federal marshal again?"

"Molly!" Cat hissed out the word with a worried glance at Jed.

Molly merely chuckled. "Fine. We'll talk about something else...like my brother's ridiculous pursuit of a certain new waitress at the Cedar Falls Inn."

Jed's face flamed, but he didn't say anything.

Since they were nearly there, Cat attempted to change the subject. "Oh, look at the roses in those urns on the front porch! Aren't they lovely?"

Molly ignored the question. "I have it on good account that Bea Hazelwood refused an offer of marriage from one of the innkeepers himself."

"Molly!" Her brother gave her a pained look.

"She broke Griff Jameson's heart into a million pieces," she continued doggedly, "and that's the last thing I'm going to let her do to you, no matter how much you fuss at me to mind my own business." Her voice was warm with affection. "You *are* my business, Jed Price!"

Despite the redness staining his features, he gave her a lopsided grin. "And you are mine."

"I am all too aware of that." She spread her hands, sounding dry. "Hence my state of singleness."

His sandy eyebrows rose. "You say that like it's my fault."

"Isn't it?" She lowered her hands to her lap. "The last time a fellow attempted to even look my way—"

"He wasn't the right one for you," Jed cut in, with an uncharacteristic burst of animation. "You'll know when it's right." He pulled his team of horses up to the hitching post in front of the inn and jumped to the ground. Then he reached for his sister's hands.

Cat studied them from beneath her eyelashes, unable to miss the adoration between the two of them. They scrapped like dogs sometimes, but they were fiercely loyal to each other. Seeing them together never failed to make her miss her own brother.

A commotion to her right made her head spin toward the new set of sounds.

A woman broke away from a huddle of men and women to hurry in Cat's direction, wringing her hands and looking tearful.

Cat frowned in concern as she allowed Jed to assist her

to the ground. It was clear the woman was distraught, and she was making a beeline in their direction.

"Miss Southerland? That's your name, isn't it?"

"It is, ma'am." Cat instinctively took a step closer to Jed. He tucked her hand through his arm and patted it reassuringly.

"I'm the mayor's sister-in-law," the woman explained hastily. "Joy Lynn North, and I was told you might be able to help me."

Cat gave Jed a questioning glance, and he nodded at her to assure her that the woman was telling the truth. Her shoulders relaxed. "What's troubling you, ma'am?" She withdrew her hand from Jed's arm so he could step away to tend the horses.

"It's our aunt in Oklahoma," Mrs. North panted, sounding a tad out of breath. "She's been ill for quite some time, and we just finished purchasing train tickets to go be with..." she paused to draw a shuddery breath, "...the family."

"I'm sorry to hear it, ma'am." Molly stepped around the two of them to reach for the woman's hands. "We will be praying for her health and your safe journey. You and your husband both."

"And the mayor," Mrs. North confided shakily.

"God be with you all." Molly squeezed her hands.

Though Cat's heart went out to the woman, she still didn't understand why she'd bothered to seek them out.

Mrs. North's features grew even more strained. "I know it's asking a lot." Her voice trembled. "But we could use more than your prayers. I could, at any rate."

"How so?" Molly asked bluntly. Though she possessed the kindest heart of anyone Cat had ever met, she wasn't one to mince words.

Joy Lynn North reached up to smooth back a loose strand of her salt-and-pepper hair. "I'll be needing a new gown before we depart. A black one if you have the fabric on hand." Meaning she anticipated being in mourning soon. "I'll pay extra, of course, if you can complete my order on such short notice. We depart in less than a week, and none of the other seamstresses in town are able to—"

"Of course, we'll help you!" Molly's expressive blue eyes widened in outrage. "But we'll not be charging you extra at a time like this. Cat and I wouldn't dream of profiting off your heartache." She directed the full beam of her righteous glare at her friend for confirmation.

"You're absolutely correct." Cat had no idea how they were going to squeeze in another sewing project, but they would find a way. "We'll do it for the regular fee. Why don't you pay us a visit after church tomorrow so we can take your measurements?"

The mayor's sister-in-law blinked damp eyelashes. "I have them written down and can recite them from heart."

Cat cast a dubious glance at the woman's rail-thin figure. Lots of people lost weight when they were distressed, and it sounded as if Mrs. North had been distressed for a good while. "It's always best to doublecheck, ma'am."

Molly started to splutter, but Cat gave a warning head shake. "You wouldn't want to be miles away, wearing a dress for the first time and wishing it could be altered."

"No, I suppose not." Mrs. North gave her a weary smile that didn't reach her eyes. "Very well. I'll call on you right after the service tomorrow."

"That would be best, ma'am." Cat politely inclined her head at the woman. "I'm staying at the Bent Horseshoe Ranch."

Mrs. North waved away her explanation. "It's a small town, my dear. Everyone knows where you're staying."

Calum MacIntyre accosted them next. He was the blacksmith's new business partner, having arrived in town a mere handful of weeks ago. A lumbering giant of a Scotsman, he boasted a surprisingly steady set of hands when it came to forming horseshoes, farm tools, fence rails, and weapons.

"Good evening, ladies." Unlike most of the menfolk in town, he generally left his head bare and allowed his thick red hair to blow chaotically in the summer breeze. Though he addressed them both, his green gaze lit as it landed on Molly. "Are you headed to the inn for dinner like we are?"

"We certainly are, Mr. MacIntyre." Cat wasn't certain he heard her, since he was so busy gobbling up her friend with his eyes. Her gaze drifted onward to the man who'd been walking beside him, and her breath became clogged in her throat.

He was none other than the federal marshal she'd been unable to stop thinking about. She drank in the sight of him — from the dust on his boots to the shiny silver star pinned to his shirt. Her gaze rested for a moment on his iron jaw before clashing once again with his hard lawman eyes.

His gaze drifted over her and Molly in a quiet, assessing manner, making her feel like he was noting every detail of their appearance and carefully cataloguing them in his mental files. His eyes were the rich shade of coffee beans, and there was no flash of recognition in them. To an onlooker, they might appear as if they were meeting for the first time.

Nothing could've been further from the truth. His clothing had dried out from the rainstorm, but he was in an even more urgent need of a change of clothing. There was a jagged rip on the left knee of his trousers that hadn't been there yesterday evening, as well as a missing button on his leather vest.

She suppressed a shiver as his grave eyes left Molly and returned to her. His mouth tightened a fraction as he nodded to acknowledge her presence.

"Good gracious, Calum. Where are your manners?" Molly chided, giving the blacksmith's arm a good-natured swat as he tucked her hand around it and proceeded to lead her toward the entrance of the inn. "Introduce us to your friend. I insist."

He tossed a smile over his shoulder at Jack Holiday. "This is U.S. Marshal Jack Holiday. He rode into town yesterday asking for a fresh set of horseshoes for his horse." He grinned down at Molly. "This is Miss Molly Price and her friend Miss Cat Southerland. They weave cloth and help keep the folks in this town clothed." As he spoke, his gaze didn't once leave Molly.

He opened the door for Molly, leaving Cat trailing a few feet behind them with Jack Holiday.

"They already met," Molly informed him flatly as she swept into the building.

"It's a pleasure to see you again, Miss Southerland." Mr. Holiday nodded so gravely at her that she doubted her presence at the inn gave him much pleasure at all.

"Likewise," she murmured, darting a sideways look at him.

He was even more handsome than she'd remembered. His shoulders were broad, and the rest of him looked equally muscular and fit.

After Calum and Molly entered the inn, the marshal reached for the door to keep it open for Cat. She was acutely aware of the brush of his fingertips against her lower back as he followed her inside.

"Are you sizing up my measurements again, Miss Southerland?"

An embarrassed titter escaped her, knowing he'd caught her staring at him.

"Well?" He gestured ruefully at his travel rumpled state.

"I'll have your shirt finished this evening," she informed him a tad breathlessly. "I'll stay up as late as it takes."

"You're very kind, Miss Southerland."

"Cat," she correctly shyly as she cast a worried look at the people crammed wall-to-wall in the dining room. "That's what everyone else in town calls me."

Tables were jammed into every spare inch available. It looked like half the town had shown up for the evening. Here and there, an extra chair or stool had been shoved beneath a corner of the tables to squeeze in an extra family member or friend. There was barely enough room for the serving staff to shimmy between the tables with their steaming platters of beef and wide-rimmed bowls of stew.

Cat's heart sank over their odds of finding any empty seats in the middle of the dinner hour.

"Don't mind if I do, Cat." The marshal's voice was as smooth as molasses. "As long as you agree to call me Jack."

While they waited to be seated, it seemed to her that he stood a little closer than necessary, employing his broad shoulders to shield her from the room full of ogling males. Calum was doing the same for Molly.

His unexpected show of possessiveness rendered her tongue-tied with shyness.

Jed Price came to her rescue, striding into the room and

heading in their direction. "This way!" He angled his head for them to follow him up a set of stairs leading to the inn's balcony seating. It was a spot normally reserved for the mayor and other important guests. Cat could only assume the presence of a federal marshal elevated their party of five to some extent. Either that, or they were the only seats left in the dining room.

At the moment, she was too hungry to care. She was simply grateful for any seat at all. In two snaps, she was seated beside Molly. Jack and Calum claimed the seats across from them. Jed pulled up an extra chair to claim a spot at the end of the table while Calum leaned forward in his chair to monopolize Molly's attention.

Jack caught Cat's eye. "It appears you're stuck with me for dinner conversation."

"Likewise, you are stuck with me." She kept her voice light, trying to quell the swarm of butterflies in her stomach. Though she could hear her brother's voice inside her head, warning her to watch her step, she felt inexplicably drawn to the marshal.

His gaze narrowed as he studied her. "I hear you're new in town."

"Relatively new, I suppose." She shrugged. "I've been here a few months."

"Where do you hail from?" He didn't hesitate to fire off his next question.

Her eyes widened. "Is this an interrogation, sir?" Her brother had coached her on what to say in situations like these. It made her heart race to realize she was finally putting his training to good use.

"Jack," he corrected. His expression relaxed. "Old habits die hard, I reckon."

"Then I suppose I'll have to forgive you," she returned lightly.

There was an answering twinkle in his eyes. "I envy you, Cat. I truly do."

"Whatever for?" She couldn't fathom what a U.S. Marshal could envy about the life of a working-class woman living in a remote cattle town.

He paused as a red-haired waitress approached them. Her expression was stiff, her nose was tilted in the air, and the cut of her navy gown was far more elegant than that of a typical waitress.

The way Jed turned red all over again told Cat she was the snobby Bea Hazelwood that Molly had been gossiping about. The same woman whom Rupert clearly sympathized with over her family's loss of their fortune.

"What would you like to drink?" She didn't spare Jed so much as a glance, making Molly's face tighten with indignation.

Jack returned his attention to Cat the moment they finished placing their beverage orders. "What I envy about you is your ability to put down roots. You belong somewhere." He looked suddenly weary. "Whereas I ride from one assignment to the next, never knowing where I'll lay my head next."

"You look as if you're ready to lay your head down right now," she noted softly, wondering if he was growing bored with her presence.

He pulled back his shoulders to stretch them. "I am," he confessed ruefully. "It was a long, treacherous ride into town yesterday, one I wasn't sure I would survive."

"Oh?" Concern for him wrenched through her.

"My horse and I got caught up in a stampede of Longhorns, but the good Lord had mercy on us. We were able to find shelter in the nick of time. Just when I thought we might actually live to tell the tale, we were accosted by the very outlaw I was sent here to track down. Came face-to-face with him, as a matter-of-fact."

"Mercy!" Cat breathed, struggling to keep her expression neutral. Anytime a person spoke about herding wild Longhorns and running into outlaws in the same sentence, they were generally referring to an encounter with one man in particular — Billy Bob Flint. Her brother. Though he was viewed as more of a hero than an outlaw by the poorest folk in the region, she doubted the marshal would view him that way.

"But all he did was relieve me of my pistols and exchange a few words. Then he let me go free." He shook his head. "I rode back out on the range today, but my only dust up was with a nest of rattlesnakes. There was no trace of the man."

Any doubts about who the marshal might be referring to fled. Fear rose in Cat's throat, nearly choking her. "Does this fearsome outlaw have a name?"

Jack Holiday watched her expression closely. "I doubt it's his real name, but he goes by Billy Bob Flint."

Molly stopped her cheerful banter with Calum in mid-sentence to gape at him. "Why are we discussing the most legendary outlaw in the west?" She shook her head in mock consternation. "I've been told by more than one rancher it's bad luck to say his name aloud."

Dread filled Cat's mouth, turning bitter on her tongue. Her appetite fled. She needed to return to her attic bedroom with haste, so she could post a candle in her window to warn the very man they were discussing. She never knew when Billy Bob would return to pay her another visit, and it was too dangerous for him to do so right now

For years, he'd warned her this day would come, and now it was here. The man sitting across from her had been sent to arrest the only living family member she had left.

Chapter 3: A Dragon Tale
Cat

C at was accustomed to bailing her brother out of his many scrapes. As a child, she'd bandaged his elbows and knees and sewn the buttons back on his shirts. Now that they were adults, it didn't feel like her sisterly role had changed much, other than the fact that his scrapes no longer involved simple things like elbows and knees. These days, his scrapes involved bullet wounds and dodging arrest.

She understood the sentiments driving him all too well. Oh, how she did! The parents he'd lost that fateful day ten years ago were her parents, too. However, she'd coped with her grief in private, shortening her first name and changing her last name to disassociate herself from the tragedy and moving on with her life. Billy Bob, on the other hand, had pursued a mission of revenge that would eventually lead to his self-destruction if she couldn't find a way to stop him.

Breaking the law was wrong, and some of the things her brother did skirted the very edge of the law. However, that didn't mean she had any desire to see him taken into custody. A man like Billy Bob would never receive justice in a courtroom. The cards were too stacked against him to receive a fair trial. For this reason, she would continue to do everything in her power to help prevent his arrest.

Knowing the man sitting across from her likely already had her brother's name on an arrest warrant, Cat forced herself to keep breathing normally. *In and out. In and out.* Bursting into tears in front of a federal marshal would only arouse his suspicions.

"Bad luck to say the rascal's name aloud, you say?" Calum MacIntyre leaned his hulking frame closer to Molly, resting his elbows on the table and looking intrigued. "Tell me more about this notorious cowboy."

"Outlaw," Jack corrected coolly.

"Some call him that. It's true. But others?" Molly shrugged her slender shoulders. Her expression was teasing and her tone hushed as she divulged in her most mysterious voice, "The truth is, he's more legend than man in this part of the country."

"Oh, he's very much a man. I can personally vouch for that." Jack gave her a look of disgust, as if he couldn't believe what he was hearing.

Jed Price snorted. "There's no point in trying to stop her, Marshal. Though my sister and I have never met the man, she's one of the rogue's biggest fans."

"Only because he's done so much good." She tossed her head at the marshal, looking like she was bracing for him to challenge her.

His expression didn't change. "Is that so?"

Cat couldn't tell if he was truly interested in the tale, or simply on another one of his interrogations.

Molly continued airily, "If you want to hear my story, Marshal, you'll have to ask me nicer than that."

Calum guffawed as if it was the greatest jest he'd heard in his life. "You heard her, my friend."

Instead of looking offended, Jack spread his hands in surrender. "Please, ma'am, will you regale us with your story about this local legend, as you call him?"

Molly gave an indignant flounce in her seat, pouting prettily at him. "Why should I tell you anything, if all you plan to do is arrest him?"

"Molly," her brother groaned.

Jack's eyes twinkled. "Who said anything about arresting him? All I said was that I was sent to track him down. I apologize for the confusion and promise to keep an open mind about this legendary cowboy."

She blinked at him for a few seconds, as if trying to decide if his apology was worthy of her acceptance. Then she launched back into her story with more gusto than before. "Once upon a time, there was a farm boy who was half cowboy and half Comanche. He lived with his parents and sister on one of the most fertile stretches of farmland. It was located directly on top of a river delta. It was said that the soil was so rich that a person could close their eyes, throw a handful of seeds in the air, and a fully ripe crop would spring forth the moment the seeds hit the ground." She paused to give Jack a hard stare, silently daring him to contradict her again.

His lips twitched. "I'm all ears. Do go on."

Cat bit her lower lip to smother a nervous giggle while her insides quaked in anticipation of what her friend might say next. Molly could be woefully unpredictable at times, but she was loyal and trustworthy. Whatever she had to say, it wouldn't involve giving away Cat's deepest, darkest secret to the man who was eagerly awaiting the rest of her story.

She had no doubt that Molly had long since guessed the truth about who the sister in her story was.

With a small harrumph, Molly launched into the next part of her tale. "According to the legend, an army of dragons flew past the lad's family's farm. After seeing how lush the crops were, they decided to remain there and make it their home. Instead of asking to purchase the property for a fair price, however, they waited until the family was asleep in their beds. Then they used their fiery breath to burn down the entire farm, not realizing the young lad had convinced his sister to sneak out of the house with him for a late-night fishing trip. When the two children returned home, they found the dragons eating their family's livestock and crops and feasting on the bones of their parents."

Cat watched Jack from beneath her lashes, feeling a thrill of hope when his expression grew dark.

"Though the children were beside themselves with grief," Molly continued grimly, "they were too small to fight back and too terrified to make a sound. Instead, they hid from the dragons in the surrounding mountains. Though years passed, the boy never forgave the dragons and never forgot the horrible wrong they'd done to his family. And as all small lads eventually do..." Molly raised a delicate finger and met their gazes one-by-one before continuing, "he grew up. The goodness that had once filled his heart was replaced with bitterness and the desire for revenge. He came up with a plan to take back what lawfully belonged to his family."

Cat wrung her hands in her lap. Though she'd heard Molly tell the story a number of times, it never got any easier to listen to. It was all she could do not to dissolve into a puddle of tears as her friend's words stirred up memories almost too painful to bear.

Molly reached beneath the table for one of Cat's hands,

squeezing it tightly as she continued. "The boy commenced his plan for revenge by plucking a single wild Longhorn from the open rangeland where his family had once grazed their herd. When no one raised a hue and cry over it, he increased his next taking to two wild Longhorns and two wild Mustangs. Still the dragons didn't seem to notice his presence or what he'd done. He delivered the liberated animals to families in need — to the elderly, to widows, to the weak and the downtrodden. As time passed, his thirst for revenge grew. Soon he was taking dozens of animals per night — all from the wild animals that roamed the country-side, mind you. The dragons finally noticed the dwindling number of animals roaming the open rangeland and launched a mission of their own to discover who'd been rounding up so many of the wild animals." She paused dramatically.

Jack looked intrigued. "Did they find the cowboy?"

Calum gave a loud chortle, looking ready to break into a full Scottish Jig.

Cat jolted in surprise, but his outburst had nothing to do with Molly's story. His excitement had everything to do with Bea Hazelwood returning with a heaping platter of food to set on their table.

Molly clapped in appreciation, and Cat sent up a silent prayer of gratitude for the timely interruption. Though Molly had carefully cloaked Billy Bob's story inside an entertaining tale about dragons, the part about her and Billy Bob's parents' wrongful deaths never failed to unleash a torrent of fresh grief inside her. Surveying the sumptuous platter of food eased some of the tightness in her throat.

There were medallion-sized steaks topped with caramelized onions, along with slices of glazed turkey and mutton. Diced potatoes, sweet potatoes, carrots, beets, and zucchini formed the outer perimeter of the platter in shades of white, gold, orange, purple, and green.

Jed inclined his head gallantly at their waitress. "You've outdone yourself this evening, Miss Hazelwood. This is a feast fit for royalty."

She gave a sniff of disdain. "All I did was serve your table, sir. The credit goes to our cooking staff."

He nodded in agreement, clearly feeling chastised.

Molly watched their exchange, looking ready to breathe fire on their hostess like the dragons in her story.

Jack broke the awkward silence. "Shall we say grace and dig in?"

Cat hugged him with her eyes, and he winked back. Then he bowed his head and said grace over the food. By the time they opened their eyes, Miss Hazelwood had disappeared.

Jed looked longingly around the room in search of her, but she must have returned to the kitchen. He forced a smile and returned his attention to his sister. Moments later, his smile no longer looked forced. There was nothing he wouldn't do for his sister. He adored and protected her openly with every ounce of energy in his broad shoulders and strong, corded arms. In a similar manner, Billy Bob watched over *his* sister from the shadows. Very few people in the world knew he was related to Cat. It wasn't until she'd met the Price siblings that she realized just how much Billy Bob's quest for revenge had cost them.

Everyone at the table lifted their forks, claiming generous portions from the platter of food in front of them.

Cat soon discovered she still had an appetite after all. She closed her eyes to savor the sweetness of the potatoes and carrots. They practically melted in her mouth, sliding warmly down her throat afterward. Opening her eyes, she nudged Molly with her elbow. "Thank you for inviting me to dinner. Everything is so delicious."

"You're welcome, my friend." Molly's whole face lit up, though her gaze held a somber note of understanding. Somehow, she'd understood that Cat hadn't truly wanted to spend the rest of the evening alone.

"I'd better slow down before I pop." Jack laid down his napkin and pushed his chair an inch or two from the table. "I haven't enjoyed a warm meal since..." He was silent for a moment. "Suffice to say, it's been a while."

His russet gaze darkened with an emotion Cat couldn't describe as he caught her eye again. "It's also been a while since I've enjoyed such good company."

She blushed. "You're very kind." She longed to borrow a few ounces of Molly's confidence and witty repartee. Unfortunately, her solitary existence hadn't left much time for honing her social skills. She was more accustomed to plain speaking with the working-class men and women she spent most of her time conversing with.

Oh, for the skill of engaging in small talk! She found herself wishing she could spend a few days in attendance at the Cedar Falls Finishing School for Young Ladies. However, that wasn't possible at her age.

Instead, she blurted, "How long do you plan to remain in town, Marshal?"

"Jack," he reminded gently. "I will stay as long as it takes to complete my current assignment."

Of tracking down my brother.

So, he was staying. That answered the most pressing question Billy Bob would ply her with upon his return. "I hope you enjoy your stay. You'll be residing at the inn, I presume?"

He exchanged a knowing look with Calum. "I am,

though this fellow kindly offered me a room over the blacksmith's shop. He also offered me a stall in their barn for my horse."

"The shop actually belongs to my partner, Wyatt James," Calum said quickly, "along with the room above it. However, he likes the idea as much as I do of having a lawman guarding the shop at night." His expression darkened a few degrees. "Unfortunately, we weren't able to convince him."

Jack look surprised by his vehemence, but he didn't say anything.

Molly batted her eyelashes at Calum, clearly attempting to lighten the direction their conversation had taken. "It was an extra kind offer, since you're staying over the shop yourself. I'm sure the marshal appreciates your willingness to share your quarters with him. You're a good man, Calum MacIntyre!"

His expression cleared. While he beamed his thanks at her, she nudged Cat's boot with her toe, indicating she was ready to bring their dinner engagement to a close. They stood at the same time.

The three men at their table shot to their feet. Calum offered them a princely bow. "Allow me to escort you to your wagon."

"I'm sure Jed wouldn't mind a little assistance while he wrestles with the horses," Molly returned breezily. She lifted her skirt and glided toward the stairs while her brother paid for their meal.

Calum quickly dropped a few coins on the table to contribute to the payment. Then he hurried to catch up with Molly.

Cat followed at a more sedate pace, and Jack fell into

step beside her. When they reached the front door, he opened it for her. "How busy is your schedule tomorrow?"

Cat nearly choked on her tongue. "I'll be attending church in the morning. Why do you ask?" She was meeting with Mrs. North afterward to take her measurements and would probably be hard at work at her looms and sewing machine the rest of the day.

He grimaced. "Though you're already working on a spare outfit for me, this one could use some mending."

Her heart sank at the realization that he wasn't referring to a social call. "I have a dress fitting appointment right after the service in the morning, but it won't take long. You may pay me a visit at the Bent Horseshoe Ranch anytime you wish after that."

He glanced down at the torn fabric that was no longer fully covering his left knee. "If you truly have the time. I never know when I'll have the luxury of crossing paths with a tailor again."

She waved away the compliment, knowing she hadn't earned it yet. "Whatever you need, Jack. I'll make time for it." For every reason she could think of, it would be best to remain on his good side.

They arrived at the wagon. To her surprise, Jack reached for her hand and raised it to lightly brush his lips over her fingers. "'Til tomorrow then, Cat Southerland."

All she could do was stare at him in amazement as he lowered her hand. Accustomed to the hearty handshakes and doffed hats of the humble farm folk, she couldn't recall a man ever kissing her hand like that before. It made her feel like a princess.

He reached for Molly's hand next and bowed over it without kissing it. "I look forward to hearing the rest of your delightful tale, Miss Price."

"Molly," she corrected, with her blue eyes widening in mock distress. "I'm sorry to disappoint you, but that's as far as my story goes."

"Indeed?" He arched a single eyebrow at her.

"Yes, indeed. The last I heard, the young man was still dueling with the dragons." She lowered her voice conspiratorially. "And winning, I might add. I couldn't spin a better ending to the tale if I tried." With a trill of delighted laughter, she allowed Calum to lift her into the wagon.

Jack returned to Cat's side to rest his hands briefly on her waistline. Then, without another word, he hoisted her into the wagon beside Molly.

Cat fluttered a goodnight wave to him and Calum. Then Jed lifted the reins and gave the order to get his team of horses moving toward the Bent Horseshoe Ranch.

Cat waved at Jack and Calum again as they rolled out of earshot. "I enjoyed your story as much as the others, my friend," she informed Molly in quiet undertones, "but perhaps it would be best not to poke too hard at one dragon in particular." She was referring to the marshal, of course. A man with the power to arrest her brother, toss him behind bars, and throw away the key.

She didn't receive the answering laugh or airy response she'd been expecting.

Glancing over at Molly, she found her friend glancing furtively over her shoulder.

Jed's eyes were on the road ahead of them. He was driving in morose silence. From his perspective, the evening had been wholly unsuccessful. Her sympathies were stirred, but she couldn't think of anything to say that stood a chance at making him feel better. As Molly had predicted, Miss Bea Hazelwood hadn't given Jed so much as a second glance. Poor Jed!

She glanced at Molly again and found her still glancing furtively behind the wagon.

Cat leaned closer to her. "What's wrong?" she hissed.

"You'll see," Molly hissed back. The next time Jed drove over a bump in the road, she used it as an excuse to jostle closer still and speak directly in her ear. "After we drop you off, go straight to your room, understand?"

Cat nodded worriedly, wondering what had her friend in such a lather. Were they being followed? Unfortunately, it was too dark to see much of anything. Clouds were festering overhead, blocking out most of the moonlight. A distant rumble of thunder hinted at another rainstorm.

Jed turned onto the road leading up to Ms. Winifred Monroe's enormous ranch home. Candlelight glowed from the parlor windows, indicating that her employer had yet to call it a night.

Sure enough, when she climbed the porch steps, she could make out the soft strains of a church hymn being played on the pianoforte. Though Winifred Monroe was a skilled pianist, she didn't play often. Cat wasn't sure why, but she didn't dare ask. Normally, she would've lingered in the foyer to enjoy her employer's impromptu musicale. However, she'd given her word to Molly that she would head straight to her attic room.

Rupert held the door open for her. "How was your dinner outing, Miss Southerland?"

"It was lovely. Thank you for asking, sir." She turned around to wave at Jed and Molly. Jed nodded politely at her, still looking discouraged; but Molly gave her a quick wave and impatiently shooed her onward.

"I'm glad to hear it." Rupert shut the door firmly behind her and locked it. "Did you run into any other friends?"

Goodness! He was unusually talkative tonight.

Cat moved toward the stairwell. "Calum MacIntyre joined us, along with the federal marshal who just arrived in town."

Rupert looked fascinated. "Did he say who he was hunting for?"

Cat's insides grew cold at the memory. "He did. It's that notorious cattle rustler that everyone is so uptight about. I don't recall his name," she lied, "but—"

"Billy Bob Flint," Rupert supplied with a nod of satisfaction. "What a pity! You'd think the government would have better things to do than go after a fella who's not hurting anyone."

"Yes, that's the man." Cat appreciated his surprisingly kind words for her brother. She moved up the stairs and paused at the first landing, hating the necessity of pretending like she didn't know Billy Bob. "They say he steals from the rich to give to the poor. As nice as that sounds to some folks, I reckon stealing is stealing."

Rupert made a grunting sound. "That's not what I heard."

"Oh?" Cat couldn't resist lingering to hear more. *I'm so sorry, Molly.* She would return to her room just as soon as the butler finished explaining himself.

Rupert waved a hand irritably. "According to the ranchers I've spoken to, Billy Bob Flint has never laid a hand on a Longhorn or Mustang that wasn't running wild. As for the cattle and horses that've gone missing here and there, they say it's not him."

His vehemence both surprised and buoyed her hope that her brother might somehow avoid arrest after all. "I hope you're right, sir." She hurried the rest of the way up the stairs without looking back. Then she quickly climbed the shorter stairwell to the attic.

Stepping inside her bedroom, she grew still in the doorway. The candle on her nightstand had a flame flickering, which made little sense. She was very sure she'd blown it out before leaving for dinner.

"Molly?" she asked quickly, then immediately felt foolish. She'd just finished watching Molly and her brother drive away.

"It's me, Cathy."

A whimper of alarm eased out of her. Immediately knowing who it was, she shut the door. No one called her Cathy Flint anymore except one man.

"What are you doing here?" He shouldn't be here. It was too dangerous to pay her another visit so soon.

"Is that any way to greet your brother?" He moved noiselessly across the room like a seasoned scout, stepping from the shadows to enclose her in his strong, reassuring embrace.

"Billy Bob," she choked, hugging him back. It was so good to know he was alive and well, despite the federal marshal on his trail. Scalding tears of relief streaked her face.

"Why, Cath!" He drew back in alarm, angling her closer to the candle on her nightstand so he could scan her features. "Are you well?"

"I am now." She dashed the back of her hand over her eyes. "I live in fear each time you leave until I see you again. You know that." She never passed up the opportunity to gently chide him for his frequent absences. Not that he had much choice in the matter, but she wanted him to know he was missed — each and every time.

His hands slid to her elbows. "Everything I do is for our family. For you."

"Maybe you've done enough, Billy Bob. Have you

considered that?" He'd certainly done enough for her. If she continued to work hard, her looms would earn enough money to make an independent woman out of her — a level of success she would happily share with him in return.

He'd faithfully served the poor and the needy, including the tiny remnants of Comanches who were scattered throughout the mountains and rangeland. He'd also protected and provided for his ragtag group of followers. Taking care of others was all he ever did. Maybe it was time for him to accept a little assistance in return.

"I've not done nearly enough." His tone was mournful. "Nothing I do will ever restore the lives that were taken from us or everything else our family lost that day. I can only hope that what I do will provide a measure of solace to others who are suffering."

It was far from the answer she was hoping for. "You say that like your mission will never be complete."

"Will it?" He hugged her again. "Should it?"

"What about you?" she protested. Wasn't he tired of constantly being on the run? Constantly being hunted like a dog?

"The good Lord takes care of me." He rested his chin on the top of her head.

Again, it wasn't the answer she was hoping for. "I think Molly suspects something," she informed him carefully. She didn't want any secrets between them.

Instead of answering, a silent chuckle rumbled through him.

"What's so funny?" she whispered.

He hugged her tighter. "Molly knew about me long before you arrived in Cedar Falls."

Cat drew back in alarm. "How?" Why was this the first she was hearing about it?

He reached out to playfully tap her nose. "Did you really think I would leave you here alone and unprotected?"

She frowned at him. "Are you saying she's one of your followers?"

He grimaced. "I don't have followers, Cath. I keep telling you that."

"How did you meet her?" Cat pressed. "Is she a friend?"

"I served alongside her brother during the war." His expression grew shuttered, telling her he had no more to say on the subject.

"So help me, Billy Bob," she seethed, "if you're putting Molly in any danger..."

"I would never do that," he ground out, looking incensed by the thought. "You know me better than that."

Do I? Feeling lost, all Cat could do was stare accusingly at him. What other secrets had he been keeping from her?

Chapter 4: Matters of the Heart
Cat

"Tell me about your encounter with the marshal." Billy Bob dropped his arms and stepped back, raising the volume of his voice a fraction. "Molly, you might as well join us."

To Cat's astonishment, her friend chuckled from somewhere nearby. "Pity! I've so enjoyed sneaking around like a ghost."

"What's the meaning of this?" Cat folded her arms as Molly stepped out of the armoire at the far end of the room. The maid's duplicity was disappointing. The fact that she was treating it like a joke made it even more disappointing.

Billy Bob angled his head at Molly as he scooted the chairs away from Cat's two looms and moved them closer together. "This was my way of trying to give you the normal life you've always wanted. If things had gone the way I'd hoped, you would've never known Molly's role in the matter."

"You lied to me." Cat wasn't ready to overlook that part. "Both of you did." Her eyes grew damp from sheer frustration.

"We didn't want to." Molly's friendly features crumpled. "Deceiving you was never the goal, my dear. Only ensuring your safety. You have to believe me!"

Do I? Sadness crashed through Cat. "Was any of it real?" Her voice cracked with emotion. "Our encounter on my first day of work here? Our instant friendship?" What about how easy it had been to negotiate a deal with Jed for her supply of cotton and wool? Exactly how far had her brother gone to spin his web of falsehoods around her?

Molly suddenly had trouble meeting her gaze. "I'll admit it was your brother's idea for me to apply for the maid position," she muttered. "And my brother was in agreement. Our friendship, however..." She shook her head so vehemently that a few wispy curls bounced against her cheeks. "It means the world to me, Cat. *You* mean the world to me." She gave him a quick glance from beneath her lashes. "Both of you do."

Cat's heart sank to a new low. "You mean Jed was in on it, too?" *I was the only one left out.* Was it because they saw her as a weak link? Someone who couldn't be trusted?

"I can explain." Billy Bob waved her and Molly into the seats he'd scooted closer together. He crouched down in front of them with an expression of deadly earnestness.

Cat woodenly took a seat, unable to bring herself to look at Molly — not even after the suspiciously damp sniffle that came from her direction. "I can handle the truth," she whispered brokenly. She'd been nothing but loyal to her brother and the memory of those they'd lost.

"Of course, you can!" Molly sobbed out the words. "Say something, Billy Bob," she pleaded. "Say something quick, or she may never speak to me again!"

A spear of moonlight outlined his ramrod-straight profile and chaotic shoulder-length hair. He looked so much like their father that Cat was momentarily transported to an earlier time. Their friends and neighbors had called their father Wild Horse Flint. Wild Horse was the name given him by his Comanche parents, and Flint was the surname of the pioneer woman he'd married — Betsy Flint, their dearly departed mother. May she rest in peace.

"This is on me," he declared quietly. "All of it. I wanted to give you a way out of the life I've chosen to live. There's no need for me to keep dragging you down with me."

"You're still my family," Cat sputtered piteously. "The only family I have left!" If the two of them didn't continue to communicate and support each other, they would have nothing. Nothing that mattered, at any rate.

"You were done traveling, Cath." He spread his hands. "You said it yourself, again and again and again."

"I did, but I would continue doing it for you. I *will* continue doing it for you." How could he believe otherwise? Hot tears welled in her eyes and spilled down her cheeks.

"But you're happy here," he pointed out in a reasonable voice. "You have the chance to grab hold of the life you've always dreamed of. You've got your weaving business. A new name. New friends. It's all I've ever wanted for you."

"I'm trying to be happy, but it's hard. Very hard never knowing when I'll see you next." She dabbed at the corners of her eyes.

"We always knew this day would come," he said slowly. "We've talked about it. Planned for it."

For a moment, she could hardly breathe. "Is this your way of telling me you're going into hiding?" Her insides grew numb. "This is goodbye, isn't it?" *Please say it isn't so!*

"I'm not sure about anything yet," Billy Bob retorted. "A lot of things will depend on what the marshal does next. He impressed me as a reasonable man. Intelligent. Bent on justice. I'm hoping we can work with him instead of against him." He steered the conversation back to his earlier question. "What did he say to you? What was your impression of him?"

Cat felt the blood rise to her cheeks. "He's a serious man. All business. Not one to smile much."

"Except when he was looking at you," Molly piped up from the chair beside her. "Or conversing with you. Or kissing your hand outside the front entrance of the inn."

Billy Bob's head jerked back in Cat's direction. "He kissed you?" The tenor of his voice rose in outrage.

"It was only the top of my hand." She wanted to shake Molly for even insinuating that Jack Holiday might have crossed a line. She clearly had no idea who she was dealing with in Billy Bob. He was more than capable of starting a war if he thought his sister had been compromised. "He was a perfect gentleman," she added. The kiss meant nothing. He'd only done it to be polite.

"He was taken with you, eh?" Her brother's voice was cool.

"I wouldn't say that," Cat protested.

"I would." Molly sounded apologetic about disagreeing with her.

Billy Bob leaped to his feet and began to noiselessly pace the room. "We could use this to our advantage."

"We only just met," she reminded. Then she launched into her recounting of everything that had happened between them. "He volunteered the information that he'd been sent to track you down."

"He told me the same thing." Billy Bob swung back in her direction.

"When?" Cat was more confused than ever.

"While I was out rounding up Longhorns." He waved vaguely in the direction of the open rangeland.

Her mouth fell open. "You came face to face with the U.S. marshal wanting to arrest you, and he just let you walk away?"

"Not exactly." His brief description of their encounter made her shudder.

"Mercy!" She felt faint. "No doubt there are laws against disarming a federal marshal." Jack Holiday had made it sound like he was seeking any information that would lead to her brother's whereabouts. He hadn't so much as hinted that he'd already laid eyes on his target, which meant he hadn't been completely honest with her, either. Nobody around her had been completely honest with her. It was disheartening.

"I left his guns within easy retrieving distance." Her brother waved away her concerns, as if it was no big deal to strip a federal marshal of his weapons. "When do you think you'll see him again?"

She wished he'd hurry up and tell her what he was up to and be done with it. "Sometime tomorrow. He's going to pay a visit after church to pick up his new shirt and drop off a pair of trousers that need mending. There's a button missing on his vest, as well, but I can fix that on the spot and send him on his way with it."

Billy Bob studied her with an expression that was difficult to read. "You should encourage his attentions while he's here."

"I should do what?" She stood in agitation. Maybe she'd heard wrong. She was exhausted to her very soul.

"Smile at him." Her brother rose to face her. "Make him feel welcome in town. Do whatever ladies do when you're sweet on a man."

"You want me to toy with his affections?" She couldn't believe what she was hearing. She would nurse her brother back to health as many times as it took, offer him refuge, and keep his secrets; but she had no interest in employing dishonesty in her personal relationships.

"Courting him might prove to be the perfect solution to our current dilemma."

"Which dilemma exactly?" Her voice was dry. From her perspective, their lives had been one long series of dilemmas.

Billy Bob pressed one callused finger beneath her chin and tipped up her face so he could meet her gaze squarely. "He has an arrest warrant for me in his saddle bag. I saw it with my own eyes."

"Say it isn't so!" Her eyelids fluttered closed against a wave of dizziness. Jack had openly admitted he'd been sent to Cedar Falls to track down Billy Bob, but he'd said nothing about arresting him. It made sense, of course, but that didn't make the news any easier to bear.

Molly's slender arm curled around her waist, holding her upright. "Billy Bob, are you sure what you're asking of Cat is wise?"

"It isn't." Cat reopened her eyes, grateful for Molly's keen understanding. "Not on any level." She didn't dare admit that her feelings might be involved, something that could greatly complicate things if she wasn't careful.

"You just finished taking me to task for leaving you out of my plans." Billy Bob pivoted away from her to resume his pacing. "This is your chance to get involved by serving as a double agent of sorts. I'll feed him information through you." He linked his hands behind his back. "Information that'll give me and my associates the head start we need while herding cattle."

"I'm a weaver!" As exciting as being a double agent sounded, Cat wasn't convinced she had the right skill set for a job like that. She pulled away from Molly. "Though I have no wish to be left in the dark about your plans, I'm not sure I have what it takes to pull the wool over the eyes of a federal marshal." Employing a little duplicity might work at first, but he'd soon figure them out.

"You're my sister," Billy Bob shot back. "We're cut from the same cloth. I say you can handle anything you put your mind to."

"Just bear in mind that the marshal we're dealing with is a good man." Molly's soft, melodic voice eased the tension in the room a few degrees.

"What's your point?" Billy Bob sent her a mocking look. "Not that I disagree. I had a good first impression of him myself."

"When your sister first walked through the door this evening, you asked her to tell you everything she could about the marshal." Molly sounded empathetic. "Though you didn't ask for my opinion of him, I'd like to give it anyway."

When she fell silent, Billy Bob gestured for her to continue.

"The fact that the marshal is a good man might pose a problem," she continued in the same soft voice.

"How so?" he demanded.

"I'll tell you how." Molly sent a worried look Cat's way. "You're a good man, and my brother is a good man. Both of you would move the mountains themselves to protect your last living kin."

He gave an affirmative grunt. "You and Cat are all that Jed and I have left."

A sudden thought struck Cat. "How did you and Jed lose your parents, Molly?"

Molly was silent for a moment before answering. "I was much younger than you when the bad things happened to my family, so I dare say my memories aren't as painful."

Oh, no! Cat abruptly took a seat. "What happened, my friend?" Her voice was barely above a whisper. So far, Molly had only repeated the lies she'd been told in bits and pieces.

Molly sank back into the chair beside her. "According to our grandparents, a group of outlaws happened to us, my dear. Not unlike what happened to your family, with one very big exception." Her gaze shyly sought out Billy Bob in the dimly lit room. "Your brother came along and helped us the same way he's helped so many other farm families. He expanded our livestock, and now we're better off than we've ever been."

Cat met her brother's gaze. "I had no idea you were doing all of that." It was a true statement. He made a habit of not telling her most of what he did.

"I know you don't care for all the secrecy surrounding what I do." He sounded remorseful. "But I had myself convinced I was doing it to keep you safe." His gaze moved to the woman seated beside her. "Until Molly came along, that is. She has some very different ideas from mine about how I should be treating my sister."

Cat's eyes widened as she turned to her friend. "You talked him into this?" *Into confiding in me at long last?* Maybe she'd been a little too hasty in passing judgment on her.

Molly nodded, eyes brimming. "I thought you deserved to know. That maybe you would worry less about him if you understood what was truly at stake."

"Worry less," Cat mused with a sigh. "I'm not sure that's possible. Even so, it's better knowing than not knowing." She reached for Molly's hands. "I'm sorry for misjudging you."

Molly squeezed her fingers. "I know how it must have looked, and it would've only gotten worse the longer we kept the truth from you." She gave a happy little laugh. "And now we don't have to keep doing that."

"Thank you." Cat meant it from the bottom of her heart. "Thank you again and again."

Molly nodded and let her hand go. "I've never been fond of keeping secrets from those we care about." She made a face at Billy Bob. "That's why I'm having misgivings about what you're proposing Cat should do next. Regardless of what the marshal does for a living, he's a man with a heart."

Billy Bob rounded on her. "If he's as good of a man as we all seem to agree he is, then he will do nothing to harm my sister. Not now. Not later. I fail to see how this poses a problem for us."

Molly shot to her feet and jutted her chin at him. "Perhaps your failure to see *is* the problem."

Cat had never before heard her sweet-tempered friend sound so righteously indignant. She was nearly as tall as he was, and there was no fear in her stance as she faced the man known as the most notorious outlaw in the west.

"This isn't a game, Billy Bob! Please assure me you understand that Cat might genuinely engage this man's affections." She jabbed a finger at his broad chest. "He's a hard-as-brass-tacks lawman. I can only imagine how far he might go to defend and protect any woman he falls in love with."

"I am standing right here," Cat reminded, tapping her

toe in agitation against the floor. Being talked about as if she wasn't in the room was almost as bad as being kept in the dark about their plans.

Neither of them acted like they heard her. "If you have a better idea, by all means share it," Billy Bob snarled. "In case you've forgotten, there are lives at stake. Property at stake. Livestock at stake. I'm already doing everything I can. Why else did you wish to drag my sister into the danger surrounding us, if not to help with the cause?"

The harsh accusation in his voice made her gasp. "She deserves to know the truth, not be punished for it! I would give up my own life before putting hers at risk."

For the space of several heartbeats, an agonizing silence settled over the room.

"Forgive me," he finally muttered, swinging away from her. "Both of you. I won't be troubling you with any more demands concerning the marshal." He stalked noiselessly toward one of the rear windows.

Molly stared at him with her mouth agape.

Dread curdled in Cat's belly. For a moment, she couldn't think past her fear — fear that she might never see her brother again. As he passed by her chair, her hand shot out to detain him. Her fingers curled around his wrist. "I'll do it." She was surprised how calm she sounded, considering how fast her heart was racing.

He grew still beneath her touch.

"You're right. I need to contribute to the cause." Remorse filled her over how much time and energy she'd spent trying to live a normal life. All the while, he'd been risking everything to protect innocent people like Jed and Molly. "If you truly think it'll help, I'll be sweet as molasses to the handsome marshal."

"Are you sure about this?" He spoke the words through

gritted teeth. "Molly isn't wrong." His expression grew bleak. "She's never led me wrong."

Cat blinked in astonishment as the truth sank home. The two of them cared for each other. Deeply. They had to. Otherwise, they wouldn't be engaged in such a passionate verbal duel.

"I'm sure." She swallowed hard. "What information would you like me to pass on to him tomorrow?"

"Cat," Molly moaned. "Please consider what you're doing!"

"I have." Cat lifted her chin. "And my mind is made up." She was every bit as clever as they were. She could do this.

"Nothing yet." Billy Bob scowled at her in concern. "For now, just get to know him better. Gain his confidence if you can. And his trust. I'll let you know what else to say to him when the time comes."

"Thank you for entrusting me with this assignment." She stood and threw her arms around him. "I won't disappoint you." *My dear, sweet, troubled brother!* Not once before tonight had she suspected his feelings might be entangled with a woman. However, there was no easy way to share his life with anyone, not with the path he'd chosen for himself.

"I love you with all of my heart," she whispered. She always had and always would.

"I love you, too," he whispered, taking a few steps back to douse the candle beside her bed. Then he was gone. She never heard the floor boards squeak or the window open and close. Only when a swirl of humid air wafted into the room did she know for sure that he'd left the house.

Cat slowly turned in the darkness toward the spot Molly had been standing. "Molly?"

A muffled sob met her ears.

"Oh, Molly!" She moved toward the sound to gather her weeping friend in her arms.

Not only was tonight the first time she'd witnessed Molly's anger, it was also the first time she'd heard Molly weep. There was no doubt about it. Her kindhearted, resilient, stubbornly optimistic friend was hopelessly in love with Billy Bob Flint. What an absolute muddle!

"How long have you been in love with him?" She rubbed a hand up and down the distraught woman's back.

It took several tries for Molly to choke out a coherent reply. "I didn't know until this very evening...until he lost his temper with me. It was almost more than I could bear."

Cat almost laughed, but it wasn't the appropriate time for mirth. "You said some things he needed to hear. He said so himself." She'd never seen anyone stand up to her brother like that.

"I should have known I was in love with him, but I didn't," Molly moaned. "I'll never be able to face him again in the light of day. Never," she repeated fiercely.

"Well, you've been very good at hiding your feelings." Cat hugged her more tightly. "You've managed to keep me completely in the dark about a lot of things." She was still coming to grips with the knowledge that Molly and Jed had known her brother for a long time. Years, in fact.

"Next to God, he's everything to me, Cat." Molly's words erupted like a geyser. "Everything I admire, respect, and adore all wrapped into one man. He's so self-less and strong, so foolishly brave." She buried her face in Cat's shoulder. "So brawny," she added in a muffled voice.

Cat gave up the fight to remain sober and started chuckling. Molly joined in her laughter. She laughed until a note of hysteria crept into her voice. Then she started weeping again.

"So, the friendly new blacksmith in town never stood a chance, eh?" Cat probably would've said anything in that moment to put a smile back on her friend's face.

To her relief, Molly snorted out a laugh. "Not at all, but he'll find the right woman. How could he not? He's like a tall mug of sunshine poured to the brim and overflowing, is he not?"

That was one way of putting it. Calum MacIntyre was as full of sunshine as the new marshal in town was full of darkness — like a gathering storm. Cat bit her lower lip and grew serious again.

"We should get some rest." She wasn't sure what Molly's plans were for the night, but she was more than welcome to borrow a nightgown and curl up on one side of Cat's bed.

"You're right." Molly moved toward the window Billy Bob had left open. "Jed's probably wondering if he needs to send a search party after me."

"Jed?" Cat crept to her nightstand, feeling blindly in the dark for her candle.

"Don't light it until after I leave," Molly pleaded.

Before Cat could ask what she meant, a whoosh of fabric met her ears. She counted to one hundred before lighting her candle. By the time the flame flickered to life, she was alone in the room.

Shaking her head in disbelief, she shut the window and went through the motions of getting ready for bed. Though she was glad to be making her small contribution to the cause, she hoped nobody expected her to climb out a second-story window. Ever!

By candlelight, she finished sewing the sleeves onto Jack

Holiday's new shirt. Then she folded it and laid it atop the trousers she'd completed for him earlier in the day. Afterward, her mind spun with too many thoughts to sleep.

At first light, she sat up in bed with a tired yawn. It was going to be a long day filled with more work than a body was supposed to do on the Sabbath. Plus, she would be engaging in her first deliberate stab at duplicity with Jack Holiday. Despite her agreement to do it, she was as full of misgivings about it as Molly was. However, she would push through them and keep her word.

She washed her face, styled her hair in a loose up-do, and donned a gown of pale pink muslin. When Jack Holiday saw her today, she wanted to look her best.

To her disappointment, he wasn't at church when she arrived with Winifred Monroe and Rupert. They never failed to create a stir when they entered the sanctuary. For one thing, the sprightly Ms. Monroe was bound to a wheelchair. For another thing, she was the oldest founding family member still living in Cedar Falls. She knew and loved everybody, and everybody knew and loved her.

By default, everyone they encountered allowed their affection for the elderly Ms. Monroe to overflow onto Cat. They just assumed that Ms. Monroe had chosen a lovely, respectable young woman for her personal companion.

If only they knew the truth! Cat quelled a shudder at the thought of what people would think of her if they knew she was kin to someone as infamous as Billy Bob Flint. Her fledgling career as a weaver would be over for sure.

As Rupert handed her into the church pew on the front row and rolled Ms. Monroe up beside her, Cat drearily pondered what it would take to keep her relationship to her brother a secret. She was going to have to be extra careful now that she was helping him. She wouldn't be able to live with herself if she slipped up and did something that would lead to his arrest.

A tall, dark-haired man stepped into her peripheral vision on the left and took a seat at the far end of her pew. She grew still at the realization that it was the same marshal who was never far from her thoughts.

Ms. Monroe leaned her way. "Methinks a handsome lawman may have his eye on you."

"Ma'am!" Cat felt a blush warm her cheeks.

"Only a day or two in town, and you've already captured his interest," Ms. Monroe continued in a teasing voice barely above a whisper.

"Oh, surely not!" The two of them were too close for Cat to pretend she didn't know what the woman was talking about. "He is a customer. That is all."

"Speaking of customers." Ms. Monroe glanced around the sanctuary before continuing. "I heard about Mrs. North's predicament."

Cat felt bad about not telling her employer about the rush order on the mayor's sister's mourning gown. However, there hadn't been an opportunity yet to do so.

"You shall sew her gown and keep me company at the same time," the elderly woman said firmly. "My weekly correspondence can wait until after you're finished with it. If anything urgent comes up, Rupert will handle it."

"That's very kind of you, ma'am." The woman was generous to a fault.

"She's an old friend." Ms. Monroe gave a decided nod. "She would do the same for me, if our roles were reversed. I certainly don't need you giving up any more sleep than you already do."

"I thank you." Cat couldn't have been more grateful for her employer's consideration. Nor could she have felt more guilty about the secrets she was still keeping from her.

Pastor Nathan mounted the stairs to the platform, preventing any more conversation as he led the congregation in an opening prayer.

Cat could feel Jack Holiday's eyes on her, though she purposely didn't look his way. She didn't want to appear too bold. It was enough for now that he'd noticed her in her pink gown. She would commence her onslaught of his heart right after the service ended.

To her dismay, the message Pastor Nathan delivered was one about trust and being found trustworthy. Her guilt escalated to new levels about her forthcoming duplicity with the marshal, but it couldn't be helped. She'd already given her word to work her way into his good graces.

Her appointment with Joy Lynn North came and went as expected. The poor woman had indeed dropped a few more pounds than she'd realized. Cat agreed to cinch in two other gowns before she departed on her journey.

She could only hope the mayor's sister was simply grieving and not ill herself, though it wasn't her business to ask. "I'll have your new gown completed in time," she assured. "Ms. Monroe is insisting that I work on it throughout the day to ensure it happens."

"She's such a dear!" Mrs. North smoothed a hand down her too-loose bodice. "She also made me promise to eat more and gain back the weight I've lost." She gave a wry chuckle. "And like everyone else in this town, I wouldn't dare say no to her."

"Nor would I," Cat murmured with a smile.

Within minutes after she departed, Rupert entered the parlor to announce Jack Holiday's arrival.

The marshal stepped into the room with his Stetson

tucked beneath one arm. His vest was still missing a button, and one of the knees of his trousers was still in desperate need of patching. His silver star, though, had been polished to a shine.

"Good afternoon, Cat." He inclined his head respectfully at her.

"Good afternoon, sir." She stood with his new outfit in hand and glided his way with it outstretched.

"Jack," he corrected quietly.

She nodded shyly at him. "There's a powder room around the corner where you can change. If you'd like to hand your vest to me now, I'll have the button replaced by the time you return."

"You're too kind." His fingers brushed against hers during the hand-off, sending a delicious shiver of awareness through her.

For a moment, she was too tongue-tied to do anything but gaze into his searching brown eyes. Perhaps it was because she still had her brother's troubling marching orders echoing in her head, or perhaps it was because of the warm way he was regarding her.

She swallowed and finally recovered her ability to speak. "I'm happy to help."

He gave her ruffled skirt an appreciative look. "Is that a new gown?"

"It is." She was tickled to pieces that he'd asked.

"Your own work, I presume?"

"It is, sir...that is, Jack."

He smiled at her use of his name, momentarily robbing her of her breath. He was even more handsome when he smiled, something she still doubted he did often.

"I'll return shortly."

She watched him stride from the room, reveling in the

sound of his husky baritone. She liked his voice and the way it resonated right through her.

When he returned to the parlor, he took away her breath all over again by how well his arms and shoulders filled the shirt she'd sewn for him. He was corded with strength.

"How do they fit?" She nearly always had to perform a few alternations at the end.

"Like a glove."

"Truly?" She gaped at him.

"Really and truly," he assured. "I hope you'll join me at the inn for another meal, so I can properly thank you for this." His russet eyes twinkled at her as he handed her his torn trousers, which he'd neatly folded for her. A few dollar bills topped the stack.

"Your payment is all the thanks I need."

"Perhaps you would humor me, anyway?" His dark eyebrows quirked in challenge.

She wanted to say yes with no strings attached. Unfortunately, there were some very big strings attached to all of her dealings with him going forward. "I would like that very much," she heard herself saying.

He dazzled her with another smile. "Then it's settled. I'll stop by tomorrow evening around six o'clock to pick you up."

Chapter 5: More Questions Than Answers

Jack

Monday evening

Jack spent the entire day looking forward to his dinner engagement with Cat Southerland. Though he'd told her it was his way of thanking her for mending his clothes, he knew it was more than that. The truth was, he wanted to see her again. He didn't have any right to, but he did. There was just something about her that drew him like a magnet.

For the first time in a long time, a feeling of discontent settled over him. Serving as a federal marshal called for many sacrifices. One of them was his travel schedule. He was constantly on the move, which made courting a woman all but impossible. Even so, the invitation to join him for dinner had more or less slipped out of him. He was going to have to be careful this evening not to say or do anything that would imply a commitment on his part that he wouldn't be able to keep in the coming days.

Before the dinner hour rolled around, he headed to the livery to rent a small buggy and a pair of horses for the evening. Then he set his course for the Bent Horseshoe Ranch. As he neared Winifred Monroe's home, the cedar trees lining both sides of the road grew thicker.

Cedar Falls was a beautiful slice of countryside. After traveling the country from coast to coast, getting to spend a few days in such a peaceful town was a welcome breather.

Well, a mostly peaceful town. According to the reports flooding the offices of his superiors in recent months, the Texas panhandle was plagued with nonstop cattle rustling. The only problem with the flood of incident reports was that Jack wasn't seeing much evidence of such activity now that he was here.

It was possible that the arrival of a federal marshal in town had temporarily halted the rustling trade. He was working on another theory, though, one in which the cattle rustling problem had been manufactured. Or exaggerated. Though there was a lengthy paper trail supporting the claims, he was having difficulty locating a single deputy or marshal whose signatures had been affixed to the reports. What's more, he was having trouble locating anyone who'd even heard of the lawmen who'd signed the reports. It was an interesting development in the case. So was the fact that he'd already crossed paths with the man he'd been sent to track down.

Billy Bob Flint was in the area, alright, proving that the recent sightings of him were true. However, Jack's gut was telling him there was more to the case than he'd been briefed on. Much more. He couldn't wait to get to the bottom of it. Next on his list was a meeting with the local sheriff, Branch Snyder.

But that wouldn't take place until tomorrow morning. Tonight, he intended to do something he rarely did — push the case from his mind and simply enjoy his dinner with Cat.

To his surprise, she was waiting for him on the wide front veranda of Ms. Monroe's ranch home. At the sight of him approaching in his rented buggy, she rose from the rocker she'd been sitting in and moved to stand at the top of the stairs.

She made an enchanting picture standing there in a gown the color of daffodils. He drank in the sight of her windblown dark curls as he brought the horses to a stand-still at the base of the stairs.

Ms. Monroe's right-hand man, Rupert, materialized to hold the reins for him.

Jack nodded his thanks to him as he leaped to the ground and hurried to the stairs to offer Cat his arm.

"Good evening, Jack." She demurely placed her hand on his arm and allowed him to escort her down the stairs to the side of the buggy. Though her smile was warm, he didn't miss the faint purplish smudges beneath her eyes. She didn't look like she'd slept well last night.

"Good evening, Cat." He gently lifted her into the buggy, completely caught off guard by the wrench of sympathy in his chest. Though it wasn't any of his business, he longed to inquire what was troubling her. Instead, he settled for asking her about her day. "How is the weaving business going?"

"It's booming," she sighed, "which is both a blessing and a curse, since I'm supposed to be serving as Winifred Monroe's companion. She was so kind to hire me, but she spends more time watching me sew and weave than anything else. Poor thing!"

Jack climbed into the seat beside her and accepted the reins that Rupert handed back to him. He discreetly slid a coin into the man's hand during the transfer and received a look of gratitude in return.

He flicked the horses' reins to get them moving. "What else could Ms. Monroe possibly want besides your delightful company?"

Cat tipped her face up to him, registering surprise. "My pen, of course! A woman of her stature has mountains of correspondence to keep up with. Instead, she's constantly encouraging me to bring my sewing downstairs into the parlor. Mrs. North's mourning gown, for example."

He arched a single eyebrow at her. "But you still hold up your end of the conversation and keep her company?"

"I do, but it doesn't feel like enough." The breeze riffled her skirt, and she slid her hands over it to hold the folds of fabric in place. From the carefully tied sash at her side to the delicate silver butterfly pin at her throat, she looked like she'd taken as much care with her appearance as he had with his. Did this mean she'd been looking forward to their dinner engagement as much as he had been? He sure hoped so!

"I beg to differ." Feeling like he was dangerously close to crossing a line, he plunged onward. "For a woman who would otherwise be alone, I think you're underselling the value of good company, which I can vouch that you are."

He had the pleasure of seeing her creamy complexion turn a rosy shade of pink. "It's very kind of you to say that."

Kindness had little to do with it. He'd meant every word of what he'd said, but he let it go.

In short order, he was tethering his horses in front of the inn and lifting her down to the ground.

She remained by his side, pressing her slender fingers around his forearm like she'd done before. He was very aware of the gentle pressure of each of her fingers, as well as the whiff of lavender and vanilla that reached his nose.

They were two of his favorite scents, notching up his awareness of her and her loveliness. They strolled in silence to the front door of the inn. It wasn't a strained silence, though, rather a soothing one.

It was nice to discover that Cat was a woman who didn't rush to fill every moment with words. She was demure, a tad on the shy side, and not given to idle chitchat. Though she hadn't hesitated to give him honest answers to his questions, she'd focused on what needed to be said without embellishment. It was refreshing.

She didn't seem to possess a single ounce of artifice, either. His analytical mind didn't detect any hidden agendas, frivolous flirtation, or random fishing for information. She came across as honest and genuine — one of those rare creatures who was exactly who she appeared to be.

No doubt some men would've found her silence off putting or insulting. Instead, he found it more intriguing than every last conversation he'd had with other women in the past. It left him burning to know what was going on inside her fascinating mind. Did she find him handsome? Or at least not repulsive? Was she pleased with his invitation to join him for dinner? Or had she simply been too kind to turn down his offer?

What he wanted to know most of all was her connection to the wily Billy Bob Flint, if any. Not only had Flint mentioned her by name, she'd become visibly upset at the mention of his name last night. Was she afraid of the man? Had they become embroiled in a heated exchange about her prices? Was there some other reason for her agitation?

They stepped inside the inn together. To his relief, it wasn't swarming with nearly as many customers as it had been the last time. Two older gentlemen were jawing over the tops of their newspapers in the lobby. Since they didn't look like they were waiting to be seated in the dining room, Jack led Cat past them to the hostess booth.

A freckle-faced teenager smiled at them. "Good evening, ma'am. Sir. Would you like a table for two?"

"Indeed, we would." Jack beamed at her.

"Follow me." The young woman flipped a white dish towel over one arm and led them to a small table on the far side of the room.

A snooty-looking waitress appeared moments later, one that Jack remembered seeing last night. "My name is Bea Hazelwood, and I'll be serving you this evening." Without waiting for an answer, the auburn-haired beauty cocked her head at them and proceeded to rattle off the evening specials — baked ham in pineapple sauce, creamy potato soup, and pot roast with glazed vegetables. Unlike yesterday, she was wearing a ruffled white apron over her gown. This evening, her gown was an elegant sage chiffon with white lace at the neckline and wrists. She was still over-dressed for a waitress, but the apron made her look a little more like a member of the serving staff.

"It sounds delicious. All of it." Jack was tempted to order a serving or two of each entrée she'd mentioned. "What sounds the most appealing to you, Cat?" While Jack waited for his dinner guest to state her choice, he wondered what the waitress's story was. The cut of her gown and faint hauteur of her demeanor made him suspect she'd recently become impoverished. Serving others wasn't something she was accustomed to doing, nor was it something she enjoyed. However, she was doing it and doing it well, which he found admirable. Had her family once owned one of the ranches that had been bankrupted by the recent rash of cattle rustling?

"The creamy potato soup, please." A note of nostalgia crept into Cat's voice. "My mother used to make it." The smile she gave their waitress was warm and without guile.

Bea nodded mechanically. "I hope our cook can live up to her recipe," she intoned. Then she blinked, as if just then realizing what Cat was inferring, and her expression grew stricken. "Your mother..." she ventured in a softer voice.

"Is no longer with us," Cat supplied with a sad smile. "If she was, she'd elbow her way into the inn's kitchen and pick up a paring knife to peel the potatoes herself."

"I'm sorry for your loss," Bea muttered. "It sounds like she was a truly lovely person."

"The very best mother a daughter could ever have." Cat cleared her throat.

"I envy you your memories, ma'am." Bea inclined her head respectfully at Cat. "The only reason my mother would ever pick up a paring knife is to carve a piece out of whomever had the audacity to suggest she pick up a paring knife."

Cat stared at her in amazement. Then she tipped back her head and let loose a laugh. Jack was utterly entranced by her spontaneity.

At first, Bea looked taken aback. Then her features relaxed, and she joined in the laughter. "May the good Lord strike me dead for my irreverence. I don't know what came over me," she added with an apologetic look at Jack. "Would you like some of the potato soup as well, sir?"

"I would." He felt morally bound to order a bowl and pay homage to the memories of the woman sitting across from him. "Along with a serving of the pot roast." He'd worked up an appetite riding up and down the streets of

Cedar Falls, questioning its inhabitants. Most of them had been friendly enough. They'd clammed up, though, as soon as they'd heard the name of the outlaw he was asking about.

Bea asked a few more questions about vegetables and sauces. Then she glided away with her head held high to fill their orders.

Jack stared after her. "She's no typical waitress. Makes you wonder what her story is." Sometimes, he could gather more information by starting conversations and letting others finish them.

Cat looked intrigued. "Are you asking as a potential suitor or as a lawman?"

The boldness of her question made him gape at her, especially since she didn't strike him as either coy or manipulative. "You are full of surprises, Cat."

"That's not an answer, sir."

"Jack," he corrected without thinking.

Her smile widened. "That wasn't much of an answer, Jack."

"It was an answer, alright," he countered. Two could play word games. "It simply wasn't the one you were hoping for."

She raised and lowered her slender shoulders. "If you'd prefer, we could talk about the weather."

He found himself grinning back at her, something he didn't do often. "I was asking as a lawman, you minx. I've been nothing but honest about my reasons for coming into town." He sobered. "The thought crossed my mind that Miss Hazelwood's newly impoverished state might have something to do with the cattle rustling problem in the area."

"Hardly." Cat sniffed. "According to the biggest gossips in town, her father made a series of poor investments."

"In what?" His instincts told him he was on to something.

"It's a fair question." She shook her head. "However, I've never been one to encourage a gossip to keep gossiping, so a mystery it shall remain." She glanced in the direction Bea had taken off to. "Unless she volunteers the information herself, that is."

He changed the subject. "Like Miss Hazelwood, allow me to express my condolences for your loss. Is that what brought you to town?"

"I suppose you could say that." Her expression grew shuttered. "My loss wasn't all that recent, though." She lapsed into silence again.

"Why Cedar Falls?" he probed.

She wrinkled her nose at him. "Is it my imagination, or has our visit suddenly turned into an interrogation?"

"That was not my intention." Remorse sliced through him. "Please accept my apologies." He grimaced. "My only goal is to get to know you better. Unfortunately, I'm out of practice with small talk." It had been years since he'd last bared his soul like this to anyone.

Her lips twitched. "That certainly puts things in a different light. Perhaps I could keep that in mind while you ask me another question."

He spread his hands, meeting her gaze humbly. "I'm interested in your story. That is all. I'm happy to share mine in return."

"There's not much to tell, I'm afraid." She gave him a wry look. "My brother and I were orphaned during our teens. Ever since then, he's been range riding wherever the wind blows him," the way she glanced away from him told him she was skirting the full truth about the matter, "and I've been looking for a place to put down roots. It felt like

Divine intervention when Winifred Monroe offered to hire me as her companion, and here I am." She met his gaze fully again. "I spend my days keeping one of the kindest women in the world company. I spend my evenings and weekends sewing and weaving, and that's the extent of my tale."

He doubted that was the case, but he let it go. "My story is shorter than yours." He leaned closer to her. "I lost my mother when I was too young to remember her, and I was raised by a father who wore the same badge I now wear. I grew up on the road in the care of one kind soul after another — from boarding house proprietresses to members of the ladies' church auxiliary. After my father perished in the line of duty, I picked up his badge and continued his quest for justice. There's a little more to the story, but those are the highlights."

"And now you're on the trail of one of the most legendary bandits in the country." Sympathy warmed her gaze, soothing the deepest, darkest parts of him. "You live a far more exciting life than I do, Jack Holiday."

"Not so much lately." He drummed his fingers on the table. "As soon as the locals find out who I'm tracking, they lose all interest in talking."

Her smile grew strained. "Maybe it's because you're not asking them the right questions."

Her statement held him riveted. "I'm all ears, Cat." If she was willing to share her insight about the citizens of Cedar Falls, he would be eternally grateful.

"Do you really need me to spell it out for you?"

"Yes, please."

"They love the man you're trying to arrest, Jack. Or at least the idea of him."

"Why?" He leaned closer, anxious to hear her perspective on the matter.

"He's their hero." She waved her hands expressively. "He rounds up wild Longhorns and Mustangs from the open range and herds them into the barnyards of the poorest citizens. To everyone who's been wronged by—" She abruptly broke off the rest of what she was about to say.

"Who's harming them, Cat? I need to know, so I can help these people," he begged quietly. Her story contradicted nearly everything written in the reports that had been handed to him. However, he was inclined to believe her. He certainly wanted to.

She frowned thoughtfully at him. "I thought you were only here to arrest Billy Bob Flint."

"I'm here in the name of justice," he protested. "I follow the evidence wherever it leads."

"Then start asking the right questions," she repeated with energy. "Ask the townsfolk what the man you're trying to arrest has done for them, their families, their homes, and their livelihoods."

His fingers itched to reach across the table and cover her hand with his. "I will ask them exactly that." Their gazes met and held for a tension-charged moment.

She anxiously searched his features, making him long to reassure her. However, he wasn't sure what she was hoping to hear from him. He sensed that she knew more about Billy Bob Flint than she was willing to share with him.

He vowed on the spot to win her trust enough to hear the rest of her story.

Bea arrived with steaming bowls of potato soup and served them with a much kinder expression than before. "One of the innkeepers overheard me mention your late mother's recipe to our cook, and he insisted that your bowl of soup will be on the house, ma'am."

"Please give him my kindest thanks." Cat's voice grew tremulous.

"You may thank him yourself." The color in Bea's cheeks deepened. "He's on his way to your table to greet you, ma'am."

"Cat," Cat said quickly, holding out a hand to Bea.

Bea eyed her outstretched hand before reaching hesitantly for it. "Bea." For the first time during her service to their table this evening, she looked uncertain.

The way Cat heartily shook her hand, however, seemed to set her at ease. She walked away, mumbling something about fetching Jack's pot roast.

He stared after her in bemusement. "I think you just made a new friend."

"Good." Cat sounded satisfied. "Ms. Monroe's butler seemed to think she could use one."

He bent his head to say grace over their food, hoping they, too, would become friends. Part of him, though, wasn't sure if friendship would be enough to satisfy the restlessness her presence stirred in him. As he raised his head, he saw a rugged cowboy striding in their direction with wind-tousled blonde locks.

He pulled off his Stetson as he reached their table to incline his head gallantly at Cat. "I'm Griff Jameson, one of the owners of Cedar Falls Inn, ma'am. Pleased to make your acquaintance."

They shook hands. "Cat Southerland, the grateful recipient of your cook's marvelous potato soup," she informed him demurely. "And this is U.S. Marshal Jack Holiday."

Jack stood to extend his hand, sizing the fellow up and liking what he saw. "I appreciate your hospitality, sir." They took each other's measure.

Mr. Jameson gave him a firm nod. "Is your room to your liking?"

"I have no complaints, sir." Jack never took for granted having a real mattress to sleep on. He'd spent too many nights beneath the stars.

"Good." Griff Jameson looked pleased. "I'd appreciate the opportunity to speak with you sometime during your stay."

Jack's interest was piqued. "Absolutely, sir!" If it weren't for his lovely dinner companion, he would've offered to meet right now.

"Just let the front desk know when you're available for a visit." Mr. Jameson angled his head toward the reception booth in the adjoining foyer. "One of my staff members will escort you to my office."

"I look forward to speaking with you." Jack shook his hand again and took his seat.

As the innkeeper strode away, Cat picked up her spoon and plunged it into her soup. "I'm not the only one who just made a new friend."

"Speaking of friends..." He hated fishing for more information, but it was ingrained into his nature to constantly be cataloging the details of his environment. "Your friend, Molly, sure knows how to spin a tale."

To his delight, his statement brought a smile to her lips. "That she can." She fiddled with her cup of tea. "It's not all fiction, I can assure you. Many legends are grounded in facts."

"Like the part about the dragons?" he teased.

"More like the man behind the legend. Her stories about him get better each time she tells them."

He stirred his soup. "I'm more interested in your opinion about the man behind the legend." He lifted his spoon and took his first bite. It was good. Very good.

Her gaze dropped to the table. "I believe he's everything the legends claim about him and more." She took the tiniest sip of soup from her spoon, adopting a faraway look.

"Have you met him, Cat?"

"That's another story for another day, Marshal."

A heavy feeling settled in his chest at the confirmation that she had, in fact, met him. He should've seen this coming. "Do you believe his claim that he only takes livestock from the open rangeland?"

She raised her gaze to him. "I do."

It felt like he was finally asking the right questions. "That's different from what the reports say about him."

She stiffened in her chair. "I don't know anything about any reports, but you're the one who nearly got trampled during a stampede of Longhorns. Did you see any brands on their hindquarters?"

"I didn't have the chance to do much looking," he admitted. "At first, I was too busy trying to calm my horse. After that, I was too busy trying to breathe through all the dirt and dust being kicked up."

Cat's fine-boned features grew stricken. "You're fortunate to be alive to tell the tale."

"I agree. Makes me think the good Lord isn't finished with me yet." He was warmed all the way to his toes by her concern for a man she'd only just met.

"He's not finished with any of us," she agreed, taking another bite of soup. "Oh, this is good!"

He agreed wholeheartedly. His pot roast arrived, and he dug in. Only after their bellies were full did he begin speaking again. "Do you have any idea where I might find Billy Bob Flint?"

"Nobody does." Her smile was bemused. "If he wants to speak with you, he'll find you. Not the other way around."

It wasn't the answer he was hoping for, but it was one he could work with. *Then I'll just have to give him a reason to come find me.*

JACK LOOKED FOR GRIFF THE NEXT MORNING, BUT THE inn staff told him he was working at his family's ranch. So he paid a visit to the sheriff's office instead.

The sheriff was a silvery-haired fellow with a viselike grip when they shook hands. "I'm Branch Snyder. Heard you were in town. It's a pleasure to finally meet you." At Jack's curious look, he went on to explain himself. "I received word you were heading our way, but I wasn't given the reason why."

"As you can imagine, it isn't purely a social call," Jack informed him dryly. "I've been tasked with tracking down Billy Bob Flint."

Sheriff Snyder's eyes bugged out. "Whatever for?"

"I have an arrest warrant for him."

The sheriff removed a handkerchief from the pocket of his trousers and mopped his forehead with it. "It sounds like you've been sent on a fool's errand."

"How so?" It was starting to appear as if every person in town had a different slant on this outlaw. Even so, calling the man's pending arrest a fool's errand was a bit much to swallow. Legend or not, the man was being indicted for multiple counts of cattle rustling. If he was as innocent as everyone said he was, the evidence would stand for itself in court.

"Well, he's done no wrong that I can see." The sheriff wadded up his handkerchief and stuffed it back in his pocket. "All he does is round up cattle on the open rangeland. Never draws his weapon and never hurts anyone in the process. It seems to me that the U.S. government would have bigger fish to fry."

Jack stalked outside to where he had Larkspur tethered at the hitching post. He unlatched his saddle bag, withdrew a fistful of documents. Returning inside, he waved them at the sheriff. "Here are no less than a dozen reports about missing cattle all over the region. A dozen, Sheriff!"

Branch Snyder made a scoffing sound, slapping his hand through the air. "I've read the reports, Marshal, but every rancher I've spoken to insisted that not a one of them has anything to do with Flint."

"You, too, eh?" Jack snorted. "Everyone around here acts like the man is a saint."

"Maybe. Maybe not." The sheriff shrugged. "All I know is you're not the first federal marshal who's come grumbling in our direction, and you probably won't be the last. It's always the same story, though. All accusations and no proof. I can't rightly arrest a man on nothing more than that."

"There are witnesses," Jack announced coldly. Or so he'd been told. He'd yet to locate a single one of them in person, which was troubling.

"Produce them," Sheriff Snyder said bluntly. "That's the same thing I told the last marshal."

Jack was already working on that, so he switched tactics. "Have you, by any chance, made Flint's acquaintance?" It was the one question that never failed to make the locals turn all twitchy.

"What if I have?" The sheriff jutted his jaw. "The last

time I checked, it wasn't a crime to have a conversation with a man."

Unless he's a known criminal that you're refusing to arrest. It was noteworthy to learn that the sheriff of Cedar Falls was yet another Billy Bob Flint sympathizer. Jack's case was growing more puzzling by the minute.

"All I'm seeking is justice," he said carefully, hoping the two of them could at least agree on that.

Branch Snyder gave him a doubtful look. "I wish I could say the same about the last marshal they sent our way."

Jack gave him a hard look. "Are you insinuating the last federal marshal that paid you a visit was dirty?"

The sheriff looked disgusted. "Nobody pays me to insinuate anything, Mr. Holiday. So, unless you're looking for the truth, you're wasting my time and yours."

It felt like they were finally getting somewhere. "I have no interest in wasting your time, Sheriff."

"In that case." He stomped from the room and returned with a young deputy in tow. "This is Brodie Marks, my deputy. He'll be happy to take you anywhere you want to go and help you interrogate anyone you wish to interrogate. I can only hope you're as ready to hear the truth as you think you are."

Jack inclined his head gratefully at the burly, bearded cowboy standing in front of him. "I'd appreciate that, Sheriff." He held out a hand to Deputy Marks. "I look forward to working with you."

Brodie Marks looked like he was trying not to laugh. "If you want to get a peep out of anyone we visit, you'd best take off that badge and rub a little dirt on your clothes."

Jack shook his head in bemusement. So much for his newly mended vest and trousers. It was beginning to sound like he should've left them torn up. However, he'd come too far to give up now. He reached up to unpin his badge and tuck it inside his pocket.

"If I promise to roll around in the dirt by the hitching post, how soon can we be on our way?"

Chapter 6: Delightful Deceptions
Cat

The next day

Cat hummed a little to herself as she pushed her needle in and out of the black satin cuffs of Joy Lynn North's new gown. She was seated in the parlor with Winifred Monroe, who was cackling over a scene in the book she was reading aloud.

"You sound unusually chipper for someone sewing a mourning gown." The book in her elderly employer's hands was a newly published, heartwarming story called **Little Women** about the joys and challenges faced by four sisters named Meg, Jo, Beth, and Amy.

Oh, how Cat had always wanted a sister! "It's only a precautionary purchase, since Mrs. North's aunt hasn't passed away yet," she reminded with a sunny smile. The woman's life remained in God's hands, and what a wonderful place to be!

"True." Ms. Monroe pushed her reading glasses higher. "I still maintain you're raining joy all over the house this morning." She gave Cat a look of mock admonishment. "I dare say a good companion would share the reason."

"I'm feeling hopeful, I reckon." Cat let her sewing fall onto her lap. "I'm living in a new town, ma'am, working at a new job that I truly enjoy. I'm so grateful you hired me."

"The pleasure is all mine, my dear." Ms. Monroe thumbed through the next few pages of her book. "Would you like to hear another chapter while you help Mrs. North prepare for whatever news may greet her when she steps off the train?"

"Yes, please!" Cat resumed her sewing, thankful when her employer didn't press harder for an explanation about her giddy brand of happiness.

Rupert appeared in the doorway of the parlor. "Mail for Miss Southerland has been delivered."

Cat's heart raced with anticipation as he traversed the room to deliver it to her with a flourish. She laid down her sewing a second time to open the precious note.

It was from Jack Holiday. Her cheerful mood plummeted as she read his thanks for joining him for dinner at the inn last night. She'd been hoping he would call on her in person today.

"Who is it from, my dear?" Ms. Monroe sounded concerned.

"The marshal," Cat declared dully as she folded the card and tucked it back inside the envelope. "He wanted me to know he enjoyed our visit."

"Anything else?" Ms. Monroe lowered her glasses to pin Cat with a look infused with girlish curiosity.

"That's all he wrote, ma'am." More disappointment crashed through her. She tried to tell herself it was because she'd made a promise to her brother to befriend the marshal, and she needed to arrange another visit with him soon to

ensure that happened. However, she knew her disappointment stemmed from more than that.

The truth was, she wanted to see Jack Holiday because
she wanted to see Jack Holiday. What a pickle to find
herself attracted to the man trying to arrest her brother!
How could something so wrong feel so right? She couldn't
even call him handsome in the traditional sense. He was too
stern and resolute, too devoted to his current case, too determined to distill everything down to black and white while
the rest of the world lived in shades of gray.

She jammed her needle into the final stitch on Mrs.
North's right cuff, wondering how many dangers Jack
Holiday would face in the new shirt she'd sewn for him.
And how many bullets he'd duck while wearing his new
trousers.

"I much preferred your humming," Ms. Monroe
grumbled.

"So did I," Molly muttered crossly as she flounced into
the room. "Ah! There you are, Ms. Monroe. Cook would
like to review menu options with you."

"Of course!" A flick of the elderly woman's wrist
brought Rupert running. Cat hadn't even realized he was
hovering nearby. After he rolled her from the room, Cat was
left alone with Molly.

"I may not feel like humming anymore," Cat announced
mildly, "but my silence is better than snapping and snarling
through the house like you've been doing." It was the closest
they'd come to discussing Billy Bob since Molly's weeping
spree.

"You must think I'm a fool," Molly spat as she swished a
duster over the lamps on the end tables. The bleached
calico she was wearing emphasized her curvy hips. It also
boasted one of her own designs, a pattern of tiny teacups

woven across her bodice and down her skirt. It was a work of art that would've been in great demand in a larger town. Unfortunately, most of the citizens in Cedar Falls dressed simpler than that.

"I think no such thing!" Cat was relieved that Molly seemed willing to discuss her feelings at last. Her mournful silence during the past few days had been painful to endure. "You're my best friend, and you're nobody's fool. That's a fact."

"I beg to differ," her friend moaned, dropping her face into her hands. "I'm the world's biggest fool, Cat. A farm girl setting her heart on someone so unattainable, so heroic, so far above my—"

"Don't!" Cat leaped to her feet to face her friend, tossing her sewing aside. "Have you forgotten who you're speaking to?" She stood there, chest heaving with indignation. "My family has endured decades of prejudice because of our bloodline." Being half Comanche wasn't easy. "But you and Jed accepted us for who we are from the start. You're more like a sister to me than a friend. A sister I always wanted and never got to have, so don't you *dare*—"

"Oh, Cat!" Molly flew across the room to envelop her in a tight hug. "I think of you as a sister, as well. Your brother, on the other hand..." Her breathing hitched on a sob.

"He's a different story. I know." Cat hugged her harder, knowing that her friend would never be able to think of Billy Bob as a brother. "I know it better than you realize." And she approved wholeheartedly. The thought of being related to Molly by marriage someday filled her with nothing but joy. "I don't have the answers you're seeking right now. I wish I did, but this I know. God does."

With a strangled sob, Molly stepped back to wipe her eyes. "You know it, and I know it, but it's still hard." She sniffled loudly. "Think about it, Cat. You can hum over your sewing and meet your beau for dinner in broad daylight."

"My beau!" Cat couldn't have been more astounded. "The marshal and I are *not* courting." They'd only just met. She was mortified that Molly had said such a thing out loud. What if one of the other staff members overheard their conversation and got the wrong idea?

Molly talked right over her. "All I'm saying is you're free to court the marshal if you want to — with everyone's blessing. The entire town adores him," she declared with passion. "As for me and Billy Bob, though?" She let out an airy sound of disgust. "What was I even thinking, Cat? There's no future for us together. Not while he's consumed with redeeming every last person who's been done wrong by the same thugs who nearly destroyed your family. No future whatsoever."

"You don't know that for sure, my friend." Cat spread her hands helplessly. "I know things look impossible right now, but facing the impossible is hardly new for either of us."

Rupert reappeared in the doorway, lightly clearing his throat to get their attention. "Ladies, you have a visitor." He gave them a gallant bow before backing from the room.

A stooped man tottered into their midst. His overcoat was heavily patched, and his long white beard made him look as old as Methuselah.

Cat had never laid eyes on him before. "Good morning, sir. I don't believe we've had the pleasure of meeting." Had he come to purchase fabric? He could certainly use a new outfit.

To her shock, he straightened and stalked right up to her. He removed his raggedy hat and dipped his head closer to hers. "Look again, Miss Southerland," a familiar male voice drawled.

It was Billy Bob's voice!

Molly's stunned gasp filled the parlor.

"I came to apologize." He pivoted in Molly's direction and produced a single red rose from somewhere deep within the folds of his ridiculous outfit. Taking a knee in front of her, he held out the lovely flower. "I know it's not much, but I offer this rose as penance for my despicable behavior during our last encounter."

As she observed his humorous plea for mercy, the storm clouds in her gaze dissipated. She gave a haughty toss of her head as she accepted the rose. "Words are cheap, peasant. But a rose?" She lifted it dreamily to give it an appreciative sniff. "No woman can resist a rose."

Billy Bob continued to kneel. "Does this mean I'm forgiven?"

She tried to give him another haughty look, but it ended in a laughing sob. "As long as you don't let it happen again."

"I promise." He reached for her hand and took his time pressing a kiss to her fingers.

Her eyes were glistening with too many emotions to name by the time he stood and strode in Cat's direction. "I have a favor to beg, if you're willing to lend me a hand." He held his arms out to her.

She stepped into his embrace, fearing whatever he was about to ask would involve Jack Holiday.

He spoke directly into her ear. "I need to drive another herd past the south side of Cedar Falls tomorrow morning, and your dear marshal needs to be somewhere north of the deed when it happens. Is that something you can handle?"

"It is." She drew a deep breath, grateful he wasn't asking her to outright lie for him. At the moment, she didn't have the foggiest idea of how she would accomplish what he was asking, but she would come up with a plan.

"Thank you." He stepped back and raised his voice to include Molly in what he said next. "I apologize for the necessity of keeping my visit short, but it's been a pleasure, ladies." He mashed his raggedy hat back on his head and tipped the brim of it at them. Then he disappeared into the foyer. Moments later, Cat heard the front door open and close behind him.

"Can you believe what just happened?" Molly breathed, staring after him. "That infuriating man brought me a rose. A rose! I may expire from happiness."

"Please don't. Your friendship is irreplaceable," Cat chuckled, returning to her seat to pick up her sewing. "And don't even get me started on your weaving skills." She was secretly debating the idea of asking Molly to go into a partnership with her. The number of orders flowing in for her fabric was quickly becoming more than she could fulfill on her own. Not only did they stand a real chance of making a pile of money together, it would be more enjoyable than shouldering the weight of the business alone.

Molly left the room and returned with the rose tucked in a slender vase of water. She set it on one of the bookshelves and delicately dusted her way around it. "What were you saying about my weaving skills?"

They spent the next several minutes delightfully debating the pros and cons of going into business together. Then Ms. Monroe returned to read the next few chapters of her book while Cat resumed her sewing. The lunch hour approached, and Ms. Monroe abruptly announced that she would dine alone in her room and take a nap afterward.

Molly returned with her duster to flit like a butterfly around Cat. They debated a few more details about their proposed partnership, and she finally threw her hands into the air. "Oh, who am I trying to kid? Of course, I'll go into business with you! Everything else is just...details."

The dreams they were spinning together were interrupted when Rupert returned to announce they had another visitor. Or rather, Cat did this time.

He seemed to stand a little taller as he declared, "The marshal is here to see you, Miss Southerland."

With a cheeky smile at her, Molly dusted her way out of the parlor and made herself scarce.

Cat laid aside the bodice of the gown that she'd nearly completed. Her heart raced with excitement and nervousness as she stood to face her caller.

"Jack!" Remembering her promise to her brother, she made no effort to moderate the happiness in her voice. "How nice to see you again!"

His dark eyes glinted with appreciation as his gaze swept over her, making her glad she'd donned her newest gown this morning. It was a sky blue calico scattered with tiny wildflowers. She was testing out a new pattern and was hoping to gather feedback from any of the ladies who saw her in it.

He removed his hat as he met her in the middle of the room. "No doubt you're wondering about the purpose of my visit." He reached for her hand and raised it to his lips.

Her heart pounded harder as his hard mouth brushed against her fingers. "I should probably preface my answer by saying I only wish to hear good news today, Jack."

He raised his head to meet her gaze, taking his time as he lowered her hand and let it go. "Marshals aren't doomed to only share bad news."

"Perhaps you should tell me your news first," she teased, "and I will decide if it is good or bad."

"I wished to see you," he said bluntly.

A gasp of wonder escaped her. "To see me," she repeated softly.

"Yes, to see you. That is all." He ushered her to the divan resting near the pianoforte and waited until she sat before taking a seat beside her. "I anxiously await your verdict about whether you find that to be good news or bad news."

A wave of lightheadedness shook her. "What are you saying, Jack?"

He turned her way earnestly. "I want to court you, if you'll let me."

"Oh!" Her lips parted, but no other sound came out. *Oh, my!* She had to remind herself to breathe.

"It's a good thing I postponed my nap," Winifred Monroe announced breezily as Rupert wheeled her chair through the wide doorway. "Never fear. I am a skilled chaperone." She waved her hands to get Rupert to park her chair directly in front of them. "You won't even know I'm here. Begone, Rupert!" She imperiously waved him out of the room.

Cat's eyes nearly bugged out as she produced the volume she'd been reading aloud to them all morning.

Muffling a yawn, Ms. Monroe opened the book to pore sleepily over the pages.

"Oh, you dear, dear, lady!" With a breathless chuckle, Cat stood and hurried to her side.

Jack pushed to his feet to assist her as she helped the elderly woman stand and move to a more comfortable armchair. In no time, she was nodding off with her head tipped against the tall seat cushion.

"There now." Cat set her book upside down on the arm of the chair before returning her attention to Jack.

"Your visit is good news to me," she informed him tremulously.

He reached for her hands, but a clucking sound from Ms. Monroe made him drop them back to his sides. Apparently, the woman wasn't fully asleep just yet.

"Then we have an understanding, Cat?" His dark gaze brimmed with cautious hope.

"We do, Jack." Her heart soared at the realization that Jack Holiday was indeed her beau. She'd been a little too hasty to chide Molly for calling him such.

"I'll still pay you for the mending and tailoring you do for me," he assured hastily.

"Absolutely not!" Her eyes widened.

He scowled in concern down at her. "I won't have folks speculating whether I'm wooing you simply to avoid settling my bills."

"And I won't have them speculating why I'm chiseling a profit from a man's honor."

"Though I'm not skilled at fancy words, logic tells me you wouldn't say that if you didn't care, Cat." He took a half step closer to her, earning him another admonishing cluck from Ms. Monroe.

"You are as wise as you are honorable, Jack." She felt like she was drowning in the admiration glowing in his eyes.

"Hearing you say that makes it all the harder for me to leave your side." His grimace held a world of regret. "But duty calls. Always."

"Oh?" His words were an abrupt reminder of her promise to her brother.

"Indeed." He gave Ms. Monroe a sideways glance, as if trying to gauge if she was still awake, then lowered his voice. "It has come to my attention that a certain notorious outlaw might be moving another herd of Longhorns tomorrow."

Her insides chilled, but she forced a light note into her voice. "You lead a far more adventurous life than I do."

"For now." He angled his head toward the door, encouraging her to walk with him. "The sheriff has been dropping hints about the possibility of curtailing my future adventures to Cedar Falls."

Rupert was waiting for them beside the front door. He opened it for them and stepped after them onto the front veranda, presumably to continue chaperoning them now that they were out of Ms. Monroe's sight.

Cat caught her lower lip between her teeth. "You would truly consider staying?" Her heart swelled.

"If I felt I had a reason to." His voice deepened with tenderness.

"Be careful out there today," she blurted, hardly knowing what she was saying.

"I'm always careful, Cat."

But there were dangers, unavoidable ones, and she happened to know a thing or two about what he might be riding into tomorrow. She opened her mouth, scrambling for the right words to keep him safe while also remaining loyal to her brother.

Jack's gaze narrowed on her. "Whatever it is, you can trust me to keep your confidences."

Guilt flooded her at the realization that her forthcoming duplicity might make it impossible not to betray at least one of the men she cared for. "I, ah...after our visit over dinner, I've made a point of listening more carefully to what is happening around me, particularly when it concerns a certain outlaw." She nervously smoothed her skirts.

"What have you heard?" His voice was steady and inviting.

"I'm not certain I heard it correctly, only that it might involve moving cattle some place north of here," she lied.

He studied her in silence for a moment. "Thank you for trusting me with that information."

Oh, dear! Her gaze flew back to his. Telling falsehoods was turning out to be much more difficult than she'd imagined. She wanted to run and hide somewhere, far from his devotion which she was no longer sure she deserved.

"Everything is going to be alright, Cat." He reached for her hand and raised it to his mouth again with infinite gentleness. "I will count the hours until I see you again."

As he walked away, she stared dazedly after him. She continued to watch him until he mounted his horse, rounded a bend, and rode out of sight.

Her hands flew to her mouth. *I'm such a horrible person!*

THE NEXT DAY, SHE DIDN'T SEE HIM. OR THE NEXT DAY. Or the day after that, though she was certain he'd returned from his mission. His foiled mission, thanks to her. She knew for a fact he was back in town because Mrs. North mentioned running into him before paying for and collecting her new black gown.

He knows I lied to him, and he never wants to lay eyes on me again.

Cat wanted to weep at the quandary she found herself in, but no tears would come. She'd done what was necessary to help her brother avoid arrest. In doing so, however, she'd irrevocably betrayed Jack Holiday's trust in her.

A good man.

A man she'd grown to like and respect in the short time they'd known each other.

A man she'd agreed to court.

Living with the consequences of her duplicity was a bitter pill to swallow.

Each time she laid her head on her pillow at night, his piercing dark eyes stared accusingly at her in the darkness. There was hurt in them, too, and betrayal.

The only bright spot in her life was that Molly was in better spirits. A full week after Billy Bob's visit, she danced into the parlor and spun in a full circle. After ensuring they were alone in the room, she spread her hands wide. "The cattle run was a roaring success! Your brother is safe, and all is right with the world again."

Grateful for the news, Cat glanced up drearily from her sewing. "How did you find out?"

Molly's eyes shone like candles through her tears as she stepped closer to wave something beneath Cat's nose. "I found this on Ms. Monroe's doorstep a few minutes ago."

Clutched in her hand was another perfect red rose stripped clean of its thorns, just like the one Billy Bob had given her.

Chapter 7: Moments of Clarity

Jack

Jack Holiday hadn't become a successful marshal without allies. He had eyes and ears all across the western region. All it took was a few telegrams to a few key individuals in surrounding towns to confirm the worst of his fears.

Cat Southerland had lied to him.

There'd been a cattle round-up alright, and it had happened right beneath his foolishly blind lawman nose. However, it hadn't transpired north of Cedar Falls like her "sources" had predicted. No, indeed. He'd been played like a harp by the innocent brown eyes of a woman who pretended to be shy and a tad socially awkward like himself. A woman who'd used those carefully crafted skills to draw him into her web with her beautifully soft, heart-wrenchingly hesitant voice.

He could still feel her delicate fingers resting on his arm as they promenaded to dinner at the inn together. He could still recall the mind-dazing scent of her lavender perfume. He, of all people, should've known better than to fall prey to such an age-old trick.

Cat Southerland's loyalties had clearly been compromised by the man he'd ridden into town to arrest. No other explanation made sense. It was possible she was laughing up her sleeve at him right this second, celebrating how easy it had been to hoodwink the lonely marshal who'd been foolish enough to think he could court a woman like her. He should've seen the impossibility of a match between them from the start. She was too clever, too beautiful, and too unattainable.

He crumpled the stack of fateful telegrams in his fist and struck a match to set them aflame. The moment they were reduced to ashes, he jammed on his Stetson and headed toward the door, needing some fresh air before he suffocated.

As he passed by the front desk of the inn, the receptionist called after him, "Would you like anything sent up while you're away, sir? Fresh linens, perhaps?"

"No, thank you." Though he made a habit of keeping nothing incriminating in the room with him, he preferred his privacy over everything else. He pulled open the front door and stepped outside into the sunshine.

He squinted up at the sky, half angry at the sun for blasting so brightly while his heart was feeling so bruised. He would've felt better if a few storm clouds had been festering overhead, or if a bit of rain had been falling to mourn the loss of his fanciful daydreams. Instead, he was swimming in sunshine while he faced a bleak future on the road. Alone. Far from Cedar Falls where the loveliest woman to ever grace a calico dress wielded a pair of looms for a living.

He glanced down the street in the direction of Winifred Monroe's ranch, wanting desperately to ride out there, demand an audience with Cat, and hear the truth straight from her traitorous lips. However, nothing she said could be trusted at this point. Her answers would almost certainly be full of more lies.

Even more disconcerting was the fact that he'd made no meaningful headway on his case yet. As one of the most reputable members of the federal law enforcement community, his higher ups had been expecting quicker results from him. The turtle's pace he was currently moving at might actually get him pulled from the case.

He tried to tell himself it was what he wanted. *Let some other badge ride into town to do the country's dirty work.* Though the thought served as a balm to his stinging pride, he knew deep down it would be wrong to give up so easily. All of Cat's heartlessness aside, Jack still had no proof that Billy Bob Flint was anything more than a thrill-seeking range rider. He'd yet to turn up a single witness willing to back up the allegations that the cowboy had so much as a pinky finger in the cattle rustling business. Even more disturbing was the feeling that he was still missing something. Something big. Something that was staring him right in the face.

To clear his head, he stalked toward the livery building next to the blacksmith's shop. The scents of hay and horseflesh surrounded him as he picked his way down the dusty center aisle and made his way to Larkspur's stall. She was munching lazily on a bucket of oats, but she perked up her ears at his approach.

"Let's get out of here, girl." He saddled her and led her outdoors. She was all too happy to leave the barn behind. He leaped into the saddle and walked her down Main Street, refusing to look at the bolts of fabric on sale in the front window of the mercantile. As soon as they left the crowded downtown area, he nudged his horse into a canter.

It was a relief to leave Cedar Falls and all of its secrets behind.

As the wind flew past Jack, his temper simmered down to the point where he could think rationally again. With nearly ten years of law enforcement experience under his belt, he'd learned that every bit of information could prove useful in solving a case, even the dead ends and false leads. While he rode, he mulled over the details of his current assignment.

After spending more than a week in the small farming and ranching community, one thing had become painfully clear. Nobody in Cedar Falls was going to help him arrest Billy Bob Flint, not even the sheriff or his deputy.

Why? The question was eating away at him. Why were the folks of this town protecting a known outlaw so fiercely? It wasn't a cowed-down kind of loyalty, either, out of brutality-induced submission. It was a fervent branch of loyalty. They adored and revered the fellow like he was Robin Hood himself come to life. Jack had encountered story after story about how he supposedly siphoned off wealth from the undeserving to hand it to the poorest among them.

But there was a problem with those stories, too, because Jack hadn't found a single shred of proof that pointed to Billy Bob Flint stealing anything at all. From what he could gather, the daring range rider only rounded up the wild livestock roaming on the open rangeland. What was so objectionable about that? And if that was all the cowboy was doing, who in tarnation had sent up the false reports that he was stealing cattle?

If only Jack could catch Billy Bob and his associates in the act of herding wild Longhorns, he would be able to vouch for the man's innocence. He'd almost done so a few nights ago, but Cat had single-handedly prevented it.

While Jack was on his wild goose chase north of town, Flint had herded his latest round-up of cattle somewhere on the south side. Where had he taken them, though? With the assistance of Sheriff Snyder's deputy, Jack had scoured the nearest mountain ranges and foothills. So far, though, they'd found no clues leading to the whereabouts of the newly claimed herd. No hidden barns. No remote pastures. Nothing!

It made zero sense. How could hundreds of wild Texas Longhorns disappear into the wind? They had to be holed up somewhere while they were waiting to be auctioned off, butchered, or whatever else Flint had in store for the creatures.

Meanwhile, no one in Cedar Falls seemed to know a blessed thing. They quietly went about their business, day after day after day, blissfully unaware of the alleged "crimes" being committed right beneath their noses. They farmed their crops, sawed trees into lumber, hammered horseshoes, tailored clothing, and served the world's most incredible pot roast and beef stew imaginable at Cedar Falls Inn.

Beef! That's it!

Jack straightened in his saddle. The inn served the freshest and nicest cuts of steak he'd ever had the pleasure of forking into his mouth. Was *that* the smoking gun he'd been overlooking?

He wheeled his horse around and set his course for Cedar Falls. It was time to go have a talk with Griff Jameson about his suppliers for the inn. As one of Jack's higher ups was so fond of saying, *follow the trail of money*. In this case, Jack intended to follow the trail of beef.

Beef was a lucrative commodity in this part of the country. If he tracked the inn's meat suppliers, they might just lead to some of the answers he was seeking. It wasn't the best idea he'd ever had, but it was far from the worst one. Anything was better than sitting still and feeling helpless.

In minutes, he reached the outermost edges of the community and slowed Larkspur's speed. He dropped her down to a walk when the church spire came into view. It was the first thing he'd seen when he rode into town days ago.

Just beyond the church was the school house. Children were perched with their lunch pails on the front stairs, the hitching post, and the side lawn. From the peals of laughter and their snatching and grabbing movements, he perceived they were bartering off the most sought after parts of their lunches. A sense of nostalgia stole over him as he remembered doing the same thing a few times while growing up. Though he hadn't been able to spend more than a few months at any one school, his father had insisted on him attending class every chance he got.

He waved at the children as he clip-clopped his way past the schoolhouse. One of the boys glanced up and waved back. A dark-haired child with a jaw as stubborn as his own, he quickly returned to his game of jacks in the dirt. The thought crossed Jack's mind that he was old enough to have children of his own. If his circumstances had been different, he might've had a son that size. Or a daughter playing across from the boy, with porcelain pale features and her hair falling in glossy dark curls over her shoulders like her mama.

He rode down the street, caught up in the impossibility of his daydreams, longing for them to be true. As he approached the first set of store front buildings, a faint moan caught his attention, snapping him from his cozy reverie.

He scanned the buildings in front of him, peering down

the narrow alleys of each one until his gaze landed on a woman. She was bent over with her hand resting against the wall of the store to her left. She tried to take a step toward the street, but she stopped and moaned again.

He immediately recognized her glossy curls, slender frame, and signature custom-woven calico. It was Cat Southerland, and she appeared to be injured!

Casting his anger with her aside, he leapt down from his horse. He looped Larkspur's reins around the nearest hitching post without properly tethering her. Fortunately, she was too well trained to attempt to run off.

"Cat!" He sprinted the last few strides to reach her side.

Her head spun so quickly in his direction, she lost her balance and would have gone tumbling to the ground if he hadn't reached her in time.

"Jack!" Her hands clawed at his shoulders as she tumbled into his arms.

After days of missing her and longing to see her again, it was pure heaven to find himself enveloped in the scent of lavender once again. There was something heady and intimate about the way the fullness of her skirt brushed against his trousers. She invaded his senses and stormed through his thoughts, keeping his attention on her and her alone.

"What happened?" He spoke against her cheek, bracing himself for the worst.

"I-I need to sit," she pleaded in a high-pitched voice.

He gently maneuvered her to the porch steps of the nearest shop.

"Thank you!" She sobbed out the words, reaching blindly for her ankle.

His concern escalated to frantic levels. He covered her hand with his, attempting to palpate the bone to test it for a break. It was difficult to make any determination through the side of her black leather boot, so he loosened the straps to remove it.

"Who did this to you?" What had brought her this far down Main Street? Was she returning from a rendezvous with Billy Bob Flint?

"I did this to me," she moaned, sucking in a pained breath and clutching his shoulders as he probed the injury some more. "I walked down here to deliver some odds-and-ends mending to one of the shop owners. She can be forgetful and leave things unlocked. So, even though she was away, I let myself inside...and promptly tripped over the animal trap she'd left sitting just inside the door. It serves me right for breaking and entering, I know, but..."

"Shh!" He shushed her without thinking. "You weren't breaking and entering. You were doing her a good turn." Though he wanted to, he made no attempt to slide her boot back on. The ankle was too badly swollen. His best guess was that it was sprained. "What happened was an accident."

She struggled to sit up straighter and face him squarely. "Maybe I'm being punished. You don't know all the things I've done wrong, Jack."

His upper lip curled bitterly. Unfortunately, he knew at least one of them. He'd been stung too deeply by it to forget, which in no way explained why the current tremor in her voice still had the power to stir him so deeply.

"I deserve whatever I have coming my way," she quavered as she watched his expression change. "Every last horrible drop of it." Her eyes welled with tears of self-recrimination.

They proved to be his undoing.

"Nobody deserves to sprain their ankle, Cat. Things like that just happen." He lowered his mouth to hers. In that moment, he would have said or done anything to ease her misery.

To his eternal joy and gratitude, she didn't pull away. Her lips were warm, soft, and welcoming, though she was still weeping. Her quiet gasps of misery finished tearing through every shred of resistance he'd raised in his heart against her. Protectiveness surged in him. He'd never before wanted so badly to defend and champion, to hold and cherish another person.

Her tears didn't feel manufactured. "I'm so sorry, Jack. For everything," she wept between kisses. "I should've never tried to deceive you. My heart has been hurting ever since."

Though he still wasn't sure why she'd done it, it helped to know that she regretted her actions. It restored his faith in her integrity. Even more importantly than that, her kisses were proof that she had feelings for him. Real ones.

His better judgment fled to the point where her kisses were the only thing that mattered. He cupped her damp face in his hands, reveling in her sweet surrender.

"I love you, Cat." It was probably too soon to tell her, since they hadn't known each other for very long. With the kind of life he led, though, time was never on his side. If he didn't tell her now, he might never get the chance to.

The holler of a man had her jolting away from him before she could answer.

Jack glanced around them and discovered a small audience gathering. Shop owners and pedestrians were gawking, and a dusty farmer limped in their direction.

"Is she hurt, mister?"

"Yes, sir." Handing Cat her unlaced boot, he hurriedly stood and gathered her in his arms. He clenched his jaw, wondering exactly how much of their tryst their onlookers had witnessed. He especially hated that there were a few wide-eyed children in the mix. "Miss Southerland has sprained her ankle. We're on our way to the doctor's office now." He carried her to the hitching post where he'd left Larkspur and lifted Cat into the saddle.

"Is that why you were kissing her?" The girl who was asking couldn't be more than five or six-years-old. She was clutching a rag doll in her chubby arms. "To make her feel better?"

A pleasingly plump school teacher with her salt-and-pepper hair piled high — probably to give her a few added inches — huffed their way. Unfortunately, she arrived in time to overhear the child's inquiry.

"I declare!" She propped her hands on her ample hips, cheeks flaming with mortification as she surveyed the scene. "It's past time for us to return to our lessons, children." She clapped her hands to get the attention of the few children who weren't paying her any mind. "Our lunch break is over. Come!"

Amid a collection of groans and complaints, she herded them back toward the schoolhouse. She gave Jack a harried glance over her shoulder, confirming that he probably hadn't heard the last of what she'd witnessed between him and Cat. It was a small town. People would talk. What a mess! It was entirely one of his own making, too, but he would deal with it later. Right now, he needed to ensure her ankle wasn't broken.

He leaped up behind her on Larkspur and reached for the reins. There were so many things he wanted to say to her, so many things he *needed* to say.

She tipped her head against his shoulder with a sigh. "Is it true? You think it's only a sprain?"

Since her head was turned his way, it had the unfortunate effect of bringing their mouths within kissing distance once again. His gaze locked on her lips, making it impossible to answer her question right away. He had to first replay her words inside his sluggish brain before he could scrape up a coherent response.

"Yes. That's all it is, sweetheart."

They both caught their breath at his use of the endearment. His gaze burned into hers, making him thankful that Larkspur knew the way since his attention wasn't entirely on the road.

"I had no right to say that," he muttered. "No right to kiss you, either." He racked his brain for a proper apology but couldn't come up with one that would undo all the damage he'd done. "I'm truly sorry." He wasn't sorry for kissing her, but he was as sorry as all get out for compromising her reputation.

Her cheeks blossomed to a bright pink, then just as quickly paled. "Take me home, Jack," she ordered dully. She sat up to face forward in the saddle again.

"You need to see a doctor," he protested.

"That won't be necessary." Her voice was wooden and emotionless. "I'll bandage it myself. There is too much work to be done to languish the afternoon away like a spoiled ninny."

He wanted to argue the matter further, but she sounded like her mind was made up. It was with a heavy heart that he delivered her to the Bent Horseshoe Ranch, where Winifred Monroe started buzzing like a bee around her.

"I'll be back to check on her," he promised as he retreated to his horse. Before he returned, there was a wrong he needed to right, and he had every intention of doing it before the day's end.

Chapter 8: Digging for Answers
Jack

J ack had no idea where to purchase a piece of furniture in a town this small, but he figured the best place to start asking was at the Cedar Falls Inn. Of all the places in town he'd visited so far, the inn had the nicest furnishings. Plus, he still needed to speak with Griff Jameson.

As soon as he stepped inside, the auburn-haired waitress who normally seated him glided in his direction. It was between the regular lunch hour and dinner hour, so the dining room was empty except for a table where four old farmers were sipping coffee and gabbing.

"Would you like a table, sir?"

The regal tilt of Bea Hazelwood's head no longer struck him as snooty. There was no shame in an honest day's work, not even from a woman who'd suffered such a drastic change in fortunes. The fact that she'd managed to hang on to her dignity in the process was admirable.

"Jack," he informed her quietly. "With as many times as you've filled my tea glass and delivered pot roast to my table, it feels strange to keep tossing around titles."

She chuckled. "Is that a yes or a no on the table, Jack?"

"It's a yes." He grinned back. "Is there a chance you could send Griff Jameson to my table, as well?" The innkeeper had been asking to speak with him, but he nearly always got called away before they could have a decent conversation. Maybe now would be a better time.

Her expression grew shuttered. "I'll see if he's available. Are you hungry while you wait?"

"No, but I wouldn't mind some of that peach tea you served me yesterday."

"Coming right up, sir...that is, Jack." She left him with her head held high, looking every inch the perfect lady.

Instead of returning with the glass of tea, Griff Jameson himself approached Jack's table with it. "Good afternoon, Marshal. I hear you're looking for me."

"Jack. Just Jack," he corrected for the umpteenth time.

"I'll agree to calling you Jack if you agree to call me Griff." Griff Jameson set his glass of tea on the table in front of him. "Is your stay at the inn satisfactory?" His expression suggested he was bracing himself for a complaint.

"It is, thank you," Jack assured. "Everyone on staff has been so kind." He gestured at the seat across from him, inviting the innkeeper to join him.

"I'm glad to hear it." Griff took a seat, glancing covertly around the room. "We've had a few complaints about Bea, but I think it's more a case of her being misunderstood than anything else. Her family has been through a lot."

"I heard something about that. Be assured she's been nothing but kind to me." He made a mental note to tip her generously before he left town.

Griff's shoulders visibly relaxed. "What can I do for you today?"

"I'd like to discuss a personal matter. Someone I know is injured."

Griff frowned and stood. "How about we take this conversation to the back?" He angled his head at the group of guffawing farmers. "Not only will it give us more privacy, there's something I've been wanting to discuss with you."

It was exactly what Jack had been hoping to hear. He snatched up his glass of tea and followed Griff through a side door into the kitchen.

The room was toasty from the heat of several ovens going at the same time, and the marinade of scents filling the air was enough to make Jack's mouth water. There was meat roasting, stew simmering, and bread baking. A long wooden preparation table stood in the center of the room. Diced carrots and potatoes were piled on one end of it, swirls of onion were piled in the middle, and a bowl of meat sauce was resting on the other end.

To Jack's amazement, Jed Price was in the room with his back turned to them. He was busy pulling a large tray of mutton chops from one of the ovens. He turned around with the tray in hand and broke into a wide grin.

"Deputy U.S. Marshal Holiday," the cowboy farmer drawled, setting his tray down on the table beside the bowl of sauce. "To what do we owe the honor of your presence?"

"We?" Jack hadn't even been aware the fellow could cook. Didn't he have a farm to run? "What are you doing working in the kitchen here?"

"I'm helping fill in for their regular cook, Jumbo, while he's on a short trip out of town. Griff's sister, Paisley, and I are juggling the workload."

"What about your farm?" There was no way he'd simply abandoned his sheep.

Jed squared his shoulders. "You say that like I don't make enough to hire a set of helping hands now and then."

"My apologies." Jack held up his hands in defense. "I certainly didn't come here to tell you how to run your farm. I'm here about Cat." He wasn't looking forward to hearing what the hulking farmer said about how he'd kissed Cat down by the church.

"Ah." Jed lifted a long-handled brush from the bowl and began to paint the sauce across the chops. "I reckon it was only a matter of time before you came a-knockin' to ask questions about the town's beloved weaver."

Jack had no idea what the man was talking about. "In case you haven't heard, she's been injured."

"Again?" Jed laid down his brush and hastily untied his apron. "What did she do this time?"

Jack scowled. "You make it sound like injuring herself is a common occurrence."

Jed snorted. "That's the understatement of the century. She has the kindest heart of anyone alive and can weave a bolt of fabric fit for a queen, but graceful she is not. There's not a hitching post standing in this town she hasn't bumped into or a set of stairs she hasn't tripped up or down. I spend entirely too much time making poultices for her." He shook his head, snatched up a basket, and started throwing supplies in it. "How bad is it this time?"

Jack shook his head, feeling perplexed over seeing this side of Jed. "According to her, she sprained her ankle while breaking and entering someone's home to deliver some mending." Jed's jaw dropped as expected, making Jack chuckle. "It sounds worse when I tell the story. I should probably leave it to her to tell it her way."

"Was Molly with her?" he growled.

"She is now, and that's what brings me to the inn." Jack

caught Griff's eye to include him in the request. "Cat and Molly have their workshop set up in some attic room at Winifred Monroe's place. I'd like to purchase something she can sit on and keep her foot propped up while she's weaving."

Jed gave a disbelieving huff. "As thoughtful as that is, I wouldn't bother. Both of those women are too stubborn to accept any form of charity."

"I wasn't planning on asking their permission," Jack assured. "Though Cat's ankle is swollen pretty badly, I think we all know she's not going to let it slow her down. My biggest concern is making sure she keeps it elevated while she works. So, if you'll just—"

"I own at least a dozen pieces of furniture that meet that description here at the inn," Griff interrupted. "Walk around, Jack, and take your pick. I'll pull the wagon around front to help load it up."

"Or I can just drive it out there on my way to pick up Molly in a bit," Jed offered. "I know just the item you're looking for. I'll go fetch it now."

"Thank you!" Jack watched him finish gathering his bowl of supplies and disappear out the back door. He was left alone with Griff Jameson. "What do I owe you?"

"A long-overdue conversation. If you'll follow me to the office I share with my brother and sister." Griff angled his head for Jack to follow him. He led him to a room that looked more like a small den than an office. "I'm sorry it has taken so long to meet with you. Please." He gestured at the array of chairs in the room. "Have a seat."

"You've been busy." Jack sat on an upholstered chair with a padded bench in front of him, much like the one he'd been hoping to purchase for Cat.

"Haven't we all? You especially." Griff sat in the chair

beside him, inclining his body closer. "Which is exactly what I've been hoping to talk to you about."

Jack gestured for him to continue. "I'm listening."

Griff's mouth twisted wryly. "There's something fishy going on in this town."

"You don't say?" Jack's full attention was engaged now.

"We have cattle disappearing, Jack. Just one or two steers here and there. It's a slow but steady trickle, and it's starting to worry the ranchers."

When he fell silent, Jack felt obligated to point out, "You have a notorious outlaw in your midst."

Griff looked at him like he was crazy. "It's not Billy Bob. You should've figured that out by now."

Jack shrugged. "I have no proof that he's involved in anything illegal."

"Because he's not." Griff gestured at him with both hands. "There's your answer. All he does is round up critters that are running wild. That said," he held up a cautionary finger, "he's run across a few cattle lately that are grazing wild with brands on their rumps. He managed to lasso and return a few of them to their rightful owners, but this is bad. For him. For the town. For everyone."

"Does he have any suspects?" Jack couldn't believe he was asking secondhand for a lead on his case from the outlaw he was supposed to be pursuing.

"He does, but he won't tell me who it is. Says he doesn't want me getting involved." Griff looked disgusted.

"It sounds like good advice." Law enforcement wasn't what a lot of cowboys thought it was cracked up to be.

"He needs my help," Griff insisted. "Don't you see? Someone is clearly trying to frame him for crimes he didn't commit!"

"Why would they do that?" Billy Bob wouldn't be the

first criminal to go on a crime spree, then blame it on someone else.

"To get him out of the way so they can keep running the smaller farmers off their property." Griff's face grew red with anger. "The Flints aren't the only farm family whose livelihood was destroyed by those scoundrels."

Jack leaned back in his chair, feeling floored. "Are you trying to convince me that Flint is actually the victim here?" That was an option he hadn't considered.

Griff looked equally floored. "You mean Cat hasn't told you?"

Jack frowned. "Told me what?"

Griff ran a hand through his hair. "Like you said earlier, it's not my story to tell. I reckon she'll tell it to you when she's good and ready. In the meantime," he leaned closer still, "I wouldn't mind doing some detective work for you that'll hopefully lead to the arrest of whoever is terrorizing my friend. Off the books, of course. The way I see it, an innkeeper is in the perfect position to keep his eyes and ears peeled."

It was the last thing Jack expected to hear, but it was too good of an offer to pass up. They spent a few minutes discussing what being a "source" or an "informant" meant, and Jack left the room feeling like he was one step closer to answers.

A little later, he and Jed were riding down Main Street with a delicate sofa loaded inside Jed's work wagon. It was upholstered in a cream fabric with a floral print that Jed insisted would suit Cat Southerland to perfection.

"It's bigger than what I had in mind, but it doesn't matter as long as she likes it." Jack couldn't have been more grateful for Jed's help.

Molly met them on the front porch of Ms. Monroe's

home with a look of intense curiosity, but all she did was hold open the door while they hauled the small sofa inside.

Jed smirked at his sister as they carried it past her. "If you're in the mood to crab about what we're doing, tell it to him." He nodded at Jack. "This was his idea."

Molly pointed upward. "She insisted on heading upstairs to work."

"What did I tell you?" Jack helped carry the sofa up both sets of stairs and found Cat seated in front of her loom. She was paler than when he'd left her, wearing a pinched expression that told him she was in pain. Molly's chair was pulled up beside her, and her bandaged foot was resting on top of a pillow on it.

Molly hurried into the room ahead of them. "Put it here," she ordered, pointing at the space she'd cleared. "That way if our customers bring a companion, they'll have some place to sit."

"I'm not worried about anyone else right now," Jack retorted. "Only Cat."

She turned a dreary face toward him and didn't put up any protest when he and Jed lifted her onto the sofa and angled it beside her loom.

Jed immediately crouched at her feet to unwrap and examine her foot.

Jack took a knee beside her. "How are you feeling?"

She made a face at him. "It hurts." She flinched as Jed bandaged it in his special poultice. "You really didn't need to go to this trouble. I would've survived."

"Is that so?" Jed looked up from his ministrations and glared ferociously at her. "If the swelling doesn't improve soon, we're fetching the doctor, and that's final!"

She made a face at him. "Cranky as usual."

"Molly, a word with you, please." Jed abruptly stood

and motioned for his sister to follow him from the room. However, he left the door open, and their muffled voices rose from the hallway.

Jack was grateful to have a few moments in semi-solitude with Cat. They stared at each other for one long, tension-charged moment. Then both of them started speaking at the same time.

"Forgive me."

"I'm sorry."

Jack chuckled wryly. "May I go first? I'm afraid I have more apologizing to do than you do."

"I doubt that, but you may." She ducked her head shyly, but not before he noticed a healthier shade of color returning to her cheeks.

"When I apologized to you earlier, I didn't intend to make it sound like I was sorry for kissing you, because I'm not. I hope I'm not offending you further by admitting it."

"You're not." She blushed furiously, glancing away from him.

"I am, however, exceedingly sorry," he continued, "for being caught by a school teacher and her students. In a town this size, I reckon folks will talk." He reached for her hand. "To make things right, I think we should get married."

"Married!" Her head swiveled his way again. "If we hadn't been caught kissing, would you still wish to wed me?"

"Very much so." He wanted to lean across the sofa and hug her right then and there for her refreshing candor. "I've been looking for a reason to stay in Cedar Falls, and I found her."

"Then, yes. I will marry you." Though it wasn't possible for her face to turn any redder, she met his gaze squarely. "Now it's my turn to apologize." She drew a ragged breath.

"I'm deeply sorry for not being honest with you from the start about a few things. I, er..." She paused and swallowed hard.

"I know you've been protecting Billy Bob Flint from arrest," he shared in a low voice. "I don't understand why, but I'd like to."

"He's done a lot for this town." Cat's voice was barely above a whisper. "And he's been a guardian angel of sorts to Molly and Jed." She paused a beat. "And me."

"I figured it was something like that. At least," he amended, "I did after I had the chance to cool my head and think it through." Way down in his heart, he'd known that Cat's intentions were good, even if her actions were misguided.

"It doesn't justify the way I've been treating you." Her voice trembled. "I hated lying to you, Jack. So much!" She buried her face in her hands. "I just didn't know what else to do."

A thought struck Jack, making his insides smolder. "He asked you to lie to me, didn't he? He needed me out of the way, so he could move those cattle across the rangeland without my interference."

She nodded, giving a damp sniffle. "I won't do it again, Jack. I already told him so. No more lying to you."

He rose from the floor and took a seat beside her, gathering her close so he could tuck her head beneath his chin. "If you're afraid of Billy Bob, I can protect you from him."

Her shoulders trembled with silent sobs, making him draw back to gaze at her in concern. "Sweetheart! What's wrong?"

She dabbed at her eyes. "I said I wouldn't lie to you anymore, Jack, and I meant it; but that doesn't mean I intend to betray the confidence of someone else I care for. Please don't ask that of me."

He clenched his jaw, understanding what she'd left unsaid and not liking it one bit. Either she cared for the outlaw, or he had some sort of dastardly hold on her that she was afraid to admit.

"Is he threatening you?" he ground out.

"Absolutely not!"

"Blackmailing you?"

"Jack!" Cat's voice was sharp with warning. "I promised to marry you and never again to lie to you. Please let it be enough."

"I'm trying," he growled, leaning in to rest his forehead against hers.

When her lips brushed against his, he knew with certainty that there was nothing he wouldn't do to protect her. Nothing! He'd waited too long for the good Lord to allow their paths to cross. She represented everything he'd been longing for while hardly daring to hope for it. Love. Acceptance. Family.

A woman gently cleared her throat, making them lean back from each other. Molly had returned. Jack hastily rose from the sofa. "Where's Jed? I need to speak with him again."

She glanced happily between the two of them. "He's about to head back to town and wants to know if you'd like a ride."

"I certainly would!" He kissed Cat with his eyes. "I'll be back in the morning to check on you."

She smiled shyly up at him. "I'll brew a pot of coffee."

"You better not." He playfully shook a finger at her. "You'll stay on that sofa and rest if you know what's good for you." He jogged back down the stairs and caught up with Jed just as he was guiding the horses away.

He halted the horses long enough for Jack to climb on the wagon. "I was starting to wonder if you were going to stay the night in the carriage house or barn." He was clearly fishing for information, but Jack had bigger fish to fry.

"Does Billy Bob Flint supply the beef tenderloin to Cedar Falls Inn?"

Jed raised his eyebrows. "Yes."

"For free?

Jed returned his gaze to the road. "I reckon you're asking as a marshal, not as a friend?"

"Correct," he said tersely. "I have it on good account that someone is rustling cattle here and there, only to turn them loose in the wild. I also have it on good account that Billy Bob has been putting Cat up to lying to me."

Jed's hands jerked on the reins. "Is that what she claims?"

Yes and no. "She mostly refuses to talk about him."

"Ah."

"So does everyone else in this town." Jack balled his hands into fists. "I'd give anything to know what he's holding over everyone that has them so afraid to talk."

"Do I look afraid to you, Jack?" Jed glared at him.

Jack shook his head like a mangy dog. "Why can't anyone give me a straight answer about this fellow?"

"Maybe you're asking the wrong questions."

Not that again! Jack rubbed a hand wearily over his face. He'd come to Cedar Falls to arrest a man, but wasn't one inch closer to accomplishing that task than the day he'd arrived. It was time to figure out once and for all why Cedar Falls was protecting Billy Bob Flint.

While Jed settled into stubborn silence, Jack reviewed the scant facts of the case inside his head. Fact one: Billy Bob Flint possessed clear ties to Cedar Falls. Fact two: He rounded up cattle and drove the herds south of the town's limit. Fact three: He supplied beef to the Cedar Falls Inn and goodness only knew how many other places. Fact four: He was in personal contact with Cat Southerland and had coerced her into sending a U.S. marshal on a wild goose chase to avoid arrest. Did that mean Cat herself was the key to unraveling the mystery?

Jed dropped him off at the inn, looking displeased.

"Thank you for the ride there, the furniture delivery, and the ride back." Jack tipped his hat at him, more than ready to start asking a whole different set of questions of the next potential witness he ran into.

"I hope you find what you're looking for," Jed called mockingly after him.

Chapter 9: Secrets Revealed
Jack

J ack sent off another series of telegrams to his higher ups, digging deeper into Billy Bob Flint's case files. Since both Cat and Jed were convinced he'd been asking the wrong questions, he decided to go back to the beginning. He inquired about Billy Bob's parents — how they'd met, when they'd gotten married, what year they'd given birth to Billy Bob, and how he'd become orphaned.

He visited the telegraph office the next day and learned that two clerks had been kind enough to message him back, one from Ft. Houston and another from Camp Cooper. The details about how Billy Bob's father, Chief Wild Horse, had met Betsy Flint were sketchy. There was some speculation that she might've been the younger daughter of a well-to-do rancher. It was possible she'd met her future husband while her father was transacting business with the Indians.

The deaths of Billy Bob's parents were recorded in sordid detail. There'd been an armed standoff between the Comanche tribesmen and the Texas Rangers on the Flints' property. The reason for the standoff wasn't listed. In an effort to force the Flints to lay down their arms, their home had been set on fire. Though Billy Bob had clearly survived the ordeal, it was initially recorded that he had perished in the fire alongside Chief Wild Horse, Betsy Flint, and a sister named Cathy.

Cathy? Jack scowled at the telegram. Why hadn't anyone mentioned to him that there'd been a second child? It was a significant finding.

Cat Southerland and Jed Price were right. Jack *had* been asking the wrong questions, because it hadn't even occurred to him that Billy Bob might've had a sibling. A sibling who might also still be alive. The possibilities swam through Jack's head like an endless current.

One possibility in particular struck him harder than the others — the one in which Cathy Flint might be one and the same as Catherine Rose Southerland. Or Cat Southerland, as she was known in Cedar Falls.

It was certainly plausible that a woman who was supposed to be dead might change her name to avoid being discovered. It's what Jack would have done if he'd been in her shoes.

He stared hard at the telegram, wondering why such a vital piece of information hadn't been mentioned during the initial case briefing. Were the authorities too ashamed of the fact that a small girl had supposedly been burnt alive during the standoff with the Flints? Or was she simply too insignificant to mention? Mere collateral damage?

The reasons almost didn't matter at this point. The fact that Billy Bob had a sister, however, did matter. It changed everything! It would mean that Cat Southerland hadn't simply been protecting an outlaw from the authorities; she'd been protecting her own flesh-and-blood brother.

"Is there anything else I can help you with, sir?" The

telegraph clerk gave him an anxious look. "Did you hear me, sir?"

Jack had to shake the haze of shock from his brain before he could answer. "No, that will be all. Thank you."

He reread the message. After the fateful fire, the Flints' land and property had been subsequently confiscated by the nearest municipality and awarded to someone whose name had been redacted from the document. Or several someones. According to the second clerk, multiple names had been redacted.

Were these the dragons in Molly's story?

Jack slapped his Stetson back on and strode from the dimly lit telegraph office. He needed fresh air before he choked on the news he'd just received.

THE THROBBING IN CAT'S ANKLE WAS MAKING IT HARD to think; and when her focus was off, her weaving was off. It was frustrating working while she was in so much pain. Her ankle was too swollen this morning to fit into her boot, so she was hobbling around with the aid of an ivory handled cane. Rupert had scrounged it up for her from the dark recesses of the attic. More than likely, it was a relic from Winifred Monroe's days prior to being bound to a wheelchair, but it wasn't something anyone talked about.

The one truly bright spot in Cat's morning was the new gown Molly had gifted her. It was a lovely shade of lavender dotted with delicate ivy leaves, one of her finest works yet. Molly had insisted it would make her feel better, which was at least partially true. It lifted her spirits, even though her ankle was still going to require time to heal.

"How about some peppermint tea?" Molly's voice was

infused with sympathy as she sailed into the room with a steaming teapot.

Cat took a deep breath to absorb the soothing scent of it. "You don't need to wait on me hand and foot," she grumbled affectionately as she reached for the walking stick.

"Stay right there," Molly ordered briskly. "I'm going to do whatever I must to help you heal. At the moment, that means I get to do the pouring while you get to do the resting." She filled a teacup for her and carried it across the room.

Cat accepted it gratefully, knowing her friend was right. It was best to keep her foot elevated on the lovely padded sofa Jack and Jed had delivered to their attic workspace yesterday.

"You would do the same for me or Jed or Billy Bob." Molly's eyes took on a mischievous sparkle. "Or even Jack, I dare say."

Cat didn't answer.

"I'm your closest friend," Molly pressed. "You might as well share whatever's going on between the two of you and be done with it. I can tell your heart is hurting enough to rival the pain in your injured foot."

Cat's fingers tightened on the handle of the teacup. "He kissed me," she hissed.

Molly grew still, looking intensely fascinated, though not overly surprised.

"Then he apologized!"

Molly's lips twitched. "What a cad!"

"Then he apologized for apologizing," Cat continued mournfully.

Molly's chuckle filled the room.

Cat couldn't see what was so funny about it. She was far closer to weeping than laughing at the memory. "What's worse, a few school children witnessed our kisses, along with their hoity-toity teacher who will surely carry the tale to others. I saw the intent in her eyes, Molly." She shuddered as she recalled the gleeful *aha* glint in the horrid woman's eyes.

"I'm beginning to see the problem." Molly whirled away from her so quickly that the skirt of her calico dress twirled like a corkscrew around her legs. "Once your brother catches wind of this..." She shook her head with a baleful expression.

Cat restlessly smoothed her skirts as she gathered the courage to share the rest of her story. "We're engaged, Molly."

Molly whirled back in her direction. "What did you say?"

Cat drew a shaky breath. "Jack thought the best solution to our dilemma would be to marry, and I agreed."

Her friend gave a shriek of excitement that echoed off the ceiling rafters. "Does this mean you finally confided in him about another very important matter?" She sauntered closer with her hands on her hips.

Cat couldn't believe what she was suggesting. "Molly, you know I can't—"

She cut her off with an irritated slap at the air. "The truth about your past is bound to come out sooner or later. It would be best if he hears it from you first."

Cat's chin came up. "If you know of a way to share my real identity with a federal marshal without getting my brother arrested, I'm all ears."

Molly's mouth twisted with sympathy. "Jack cares for you. That's what I do know. Perhaps a little trust is in order between you and the man you're going to marry?"

A fist pounded on the door of their attic workshop, making them both jump.

"Er, come in," Cat called hesitantly.

Rupert cracked open the door. "My apologies for interrupting you, but..."

Jack pushed the door wider and stepped across the threshold, waving a small slip of paper. His expression was livid. "We need to talk, *Cathy*."

She felt the blood drain from her face. So much for Molly's well-meant advice, but it was too late for trading confidences. He already knew.

He glanced pointedly at Molly. "If you'd be so kind to give me a moment with my *affianced*."

Rupert's silvery eyebrows shot upward over the announcement. "I'll be right around the corner," he promised with a worried look at Cat.

Cat nodded at him to let him know she would be okay.

Molly leaned over the sofa to mutter in her ear. "He deserves the truth this time. All of it." She straightened and swept past the two men, disappearing down the hallway.

Rupert made a big show of propping the door the rest of the way open before stepping around the corner to stand vigil as their chaperone.

Jack closed the distance between them to stand directly in front of her. "Is there anything else you need to tell me?" He allowed the slip of paper he'd been holding to drop from his fingers. It drifted to her lap like a feather floating on the wind.

It was a telegram. She snatched it up and hastily read its contents. It was a brief accounting of the fire that had taken her parents' lives. She numbly lowered the telegram to her lap.

It was over.

All her years of running, hiding, and pretending...
Because of the Comanche blood running through her veins,
she was going to suffer the same fate as her parents. She
would lose everything — her position as Ms. Monroe's
companion, her weaving business, and her freedom. The
moment her mother had become the sole heir of her family's
ranch, a set of nameless, faceless enemies from the shadows
had demanded she forfeit it. Masked men had come and
attempted to cart them off to a reservation like a sack of
potatoes.

She tipped her stricken face up to his. "Now you know
everything." She couldn't run anymore if she wanted to.
Her swollen ankle had made it impossible.

"I don't, but I want to." He gingerly took a seat on the
edge of the sofa facing her. "I can't begin to describe what it
felt like to receive this telegram." He let out a weary breath.
"To know that the woman I'm about to marry hadn't trusted
me enough to tell me her real name. Do you have any idea
what position this puts me in as a federal marshal?"

She dropped her gaze, unable to face the agonized accusation in his eyes, the burning questions, the hurt of
betrayal. It was probably no comfort to him, but her heart
was breaking, too.

"Please don't pull away from me, Cat. Not this time."
His fingers closed around hers. "I'll admit I was shocked to
discover who you really are. I was hurt and angry, but not at
you."

What? His words were so unexpected that she shuddered. The last thing she'd expected was his understanding.
The realization of just how badly she'd underestimated him
slammed into her, bringing the sting of tears to her eyes.

"What happened to your family that day was a horrible miscarriage of justice, Cat."

"Do you really believe that?" Was it truly possible for a man sworn to uphold the law to find her *not* flawed for being half-Comanche...and *not* guilty for living somewhere besides a government-sanctioned reservation? She raised her head, reveling in the fiercely tender note in his voice.

"I believe it with all of my heart, and I'm going to do everything in my power to clear your family's name." His fingers tightened on hers. "My only wish right now is that I could've been a man you found worthy of being entrusted with the truth sooner."

"It was more about my fear than anything else." She drew a ragged breath. "I was afraid, because of who I am." Her father's heritage and her mother's inheritance had proved to be a lethal combination. People, whose names Billy Bob hadn't uncovered until many years later, had been willing to commit murder to take what rightfully belonged to the Flints, hiding like cowards beneath their hate and greed.

"I know that now." Jack's voice grew pleading. "Tell me the rest of your story, so I can understand."

His humble request made tears streak down her cheeks. "Billy Bob and I lost everything that night. Our parents, our friends, our home, our land, our belongings..." Her voice broke. "Mother had hoped her own citizenship would protect our family from wave after wave of land reclamations and forced relocations. It should have. I don't understand what went wrong. Maybe Billy Bob and I were simply too young to understand. All we could piece together after the fact was that allegations were levied against my parents. The Rangers came banging on our front door, and..." She sniffled and dabbed at her tears. "Father must've known the standoff wouldn't end well, because he sent Billy Bob and me away in the middle of the night. He made us pack as if we were going on a long trip. He gave us blankets and medicine, weapons, and enough food to survive for several days. He tried to make Mother go with us, but she refused to leave his side. They drew us a map that would lead us to a small tribe of refugees in the mountains and told us to wait for them there...that they would come for us when it was all over."

Instead, they'd perished that same night in the fire someone had purposely set to flush them out of hiding. Two someones, actually. Two someones who'd been severely burned themselves while trying to ensure that all four members of the Flint family perished. Two someones who continued to commit crimes in Billy Bob's name to ensure he would remain on the run and never be able to reclaim the land that was rightfully his.

Jack was silent for a reverent moment. "What happened next?"

She raised and lowered her shoulders resignedly. "We lived like gypsies for a while, tagging along with various groups of refugees, mostly Comanches and Kiowas. We were young, but we weren't babies. We could hunt, fish, trap, and grow food. We knew how to live off the land as skillfully as any adult. The biggest challenge wasn't surviving. It was evading capture." Thanks to the same two someones who constantly stalked Billy Bob and reported their sightings of the "outlaw" to sheriffs across the region.

"I'm sorry for everything you suffered." Jack reached out to touch her cheek. "I'm also in awe of how brave and resourceful you were in the midst of tragedy. Many people

wouldn't have had the heart to go on after such a tremen-
dous loss."

Cat smiled through her tears at him. "I had Billy Bob,
and Billy Bob had me. For years, it was just the two of us
against the rest of the world. I wouldn't have survived
without him, and I don't think he would've survived
without me, either." She shook her head. "We've always
trusted each other and protected each other." Her eyes
filled with a fresh round of tears. "We still do, Jack. If that
makes you think less of me, then so be it." She was
completely at his mercy, and he knew it.

She braced herself for his reaction

He sighed and cupped her face in his hands. "Nothing
you've told me today changes the fact that you're the
woman I love. The woman I hope to marry as soon as possible. The sooner the better, everything considered."

She gaped at him, unable to believe she was hearing
correctly. "You still want to marry me?"

"If you're still willing." He beheld her with tender
adoration. "Being my wife won't be easy, whether I remain
a federal marshal or accept Sheriff Snyder's offer to remain
in Cedar Falls. I'm probably the most selfish brute on the
planet for even asking this of you, but nothing would make
me happier than to become your husband."

She wanted to launch herself into his arms and weep
out her mixture of happiness and sadness, but fear still held
her back. "What about my brother's arrest warrant?" As
powerful as their love was, it didn't erase the false accusations her brother was battling. "Please don't ask me to
choose between him and you. I couldn't bear it."

"I won't." His mouth twisted wryly. "He'll become my
brother when we get married, as well as the uncle of any
children the Lord blesses us with. Understand this, though,

sweetheart. It's my sworn duty to uphold and enforce the law. I'll never ask you to stop loving and protecting your brother. In return, please don't ask me to compromise my principles for him or anyone else. When the time comes, he'll have to answer for his sins the same as any other man."

Her insides quaked at the knowledge that Jack still viewed her brother as a criminal. *The whole truth*, Molly had warned. *Tell him the whole truth this time.*

The problem was that even Molly didn't know the whole truth, and Cat wasn't sure she'd ever have the heart to tell her. Billy Bob had been protecting her and Jed from the worst of it, just as fiercely as he'd been defending all the other farmers and ranchers in Cedar Falls.

He'd been doing it for years, but maybe it was time for someone to defend him in return. "As Billy Bob's sister, I know my word will never be seen as reliable on the matter. However, I believe with all of my heart that his arrest warrant was drawn up on false charges."

"You're right." Jack's jaw clenched. "Others may not believe you, sweetheart, but I do. I will."

His impassioned declaration gave her the courage to continue. "He's innocent," she declared with years of pent up vehemence. "All he's ever done is round up the wild cattle on the open range, mostly cattle grazing near the land that once belonged to our family. Yes, it made the surrounding ranchers angry, because every Longhorn he took was one less Longhorn for the taking; but he broke no laws." He'd herded most of them into the barnyards of the struggling farmers living throughout the region. He also sold a steady supply of them at a steep discount to honest business owners like the Jamesons at Cedar Falls Inn. He'd used the money to purchase Cat a one-way train ticket to what he hoped would be a normal life for her. He'd also purchased the two looms for her.

Jack blew out a breath. "As much as I want to believe his innocence the same way you do, I'm going to need some proof. That's how this works."

Unsure it would do any good, she revealed her final secret to him. "The real criminals are Molly and Jed's parents. Molly and Jed think they're orphans. After their parents were burned in the fire, there was no denying their involvement, so they left Molly and Jed in the care of their grandparents and went on the run. In their twisted attempt to keep the farm they unlawfully acquired in the possession of the Price family, they've continued to stir up trouble for Billy Bob and me. They won't be satisfied until we're out of the picture for good."

Jack studied her gravely. "Which is why you changed your name."

She nodded. "Not in my wildest imagining did I foresee Billy Bob meeting and become such close friends with Jed, much less falling in love with Molly. It's ironic, isn't it?"

"More like poetic justice, if you ask me." Jack gave a humorless bark of laughter. "When your brother marries Molly, it'll defeat the evil her parents have wasted so many years cultivating."

Footsteps pounded up the stairs in their direction. Jack stood and turned to eyeball her latest guest, standing protectively in front of her.

Rupert appeared in the doorway again, this time with Molly and Jed in tow. Their expressions indicated something was terribly wrong.

"Calum just spotted a party of Texas Rangers riding this way," she announced hoarsely. "Oh, Cat! He said they're coming to question you about Billy Bob's whereabouts, which means..."

Jed jumped, white-faced, into the conversation. "Someone must have figured out who you are." He glanced wildly around the room, as if searching for a place to hide her.

Molly wrung her hands, moaning, "What are we going to do?"

Chapter 10: Showdown
Jack

J ack sprinted to the front window. "I was told they would be sending backup troops if I didn't arrest Billy Bob soon." He peered down the cedar-lined driveway leading to Winifred Monroe's front veranda. "I assured them it wasn't necessary. Apparently, they don't agree." He had a plan, though. And after everything Cat had confessed to him, it made more sense than ever to move forward with it.

"I repeat. What are we going to do?" Molly's voice trembled with agitation.

Jack returned to Cat's side to lay a hand on her shoulder. "A few days ago, a wise man suggested I ask the right questions, so I did. I started off by asking Cat to marry me, and she said yes."

Cat reached up to touch his hand, and he briefly twined his fingers with hers.

"That's what we're going to do, Molly." He raised Cat's hand to kiss her fingertips. "I'm going to make her my wife and give her the protection of my name and badge." It was only the first step in his plan, but it was a vitally important one. "Today, if she's willing to marry me with only one boot on."

"B-but..." Molly sputtered, turning deathly pale.

"Are you sure now is a good time for a wedding?" Jed looked as sick at heart as Molly, laying one final suspicion of Jack's to rest. "Billy Bob won't miss his own sister's wedding." He was genuinely concerned for his friend's safety.

"I'm counting on it," Jack admitted in satisfaction. "To borrow one of Flint's own strategies, you and I will send the Rangers in a different direction."

"How?" Jed clenched and unclenched his fists, ready for action.

Jack already had it planned out. As long as Jed followed his lead, everything was going to be alright. "On a tip there's been yet another sighting of him. We'll send word to one of the farmers to post a few scraggly Longhorns out there to make it look like an authentic lead."

"That should give Billy Bob enough time to attend your wedding." Molly still looked doubtful. "As long as the minister doesn't get too long-winded."

"He won't." Jack waggled his eyebrows at her, because he knew another thing she didn't yet know — that Billy Bob was also planning on getting married.

"Please assure us this means you plan to let him make his getaway afterward." Molly's gaze glistened with the brand of love and loyalty that a man like Billy Bob deserved. She was strong and resourceful. She would make him a worthy lifelong partner. His only regret about the hand he was about to play in their happiness was the sadness Cat was sure to feel over their coming separation. Lord willing, it wouldn't last forever. He would spend the rest of his days, if need be, sorting out the mess and bringing the truth to light.

He met her gaze levelly. "After a lengthy investigation, I find him innocent of all charges. It won't be easy, but I'm going to clear my future brother-in-law's name and restore honor to the Flint legacy."

CAT BLINKED RAPIDLY, TRYING TO HOLD BACK ANOTHER round of tears. Though she was grateful for the grace Jack was showing her brother, she knew this meant they would be saying goodbye for a while. He would be forced to flee to the mountains and disappear again until Jack succeeded in his newest mission. This time, however, he would be doing it alone.

Without me.

She and Molly exchanged a glance infused with dread. She could practically feel her friend's heart breaking over the coming separation.

Jack moved toward the door, donning his Stetson. "I'll meet the Rangers and head them off."

"I'll go with you," Jed said quickly. "As soon as they take their detour, we can send word to Billy Bob that his presence is needed in town."

Jack nodded soberly. "Then the rest of us will head to the church for the wedding."

The men made their exit, leaving Cat and Molly gazing bleakly at each other.

"I'll, er, pack a few provisions for your brother." Molly nodded at the other side of the room where Cat kept her personal belongings. "It's the least we can do for him." She dashed a hand over her eyes. "You keep resting. I'll be back shortly to help get you ready for the wedding."

"Thank you." Cat grimaced at her bandaged ankle. She'd be getting married while leaning on a cane, apparently, but that couldn't be helped. It was a comfort knowing that Jack would be at her side. He would never let her fall.

The next half hour passed in a flurry of preparations, during which Molly reported from the window that Jack and Jed were loading all sorts of bundles into the wagon. Rupert was helping them.

Cat frowned thoughtfully. "Do you think Rupert knows about...me?"

Molly snorted. "Of course, he does. Ms. Monroe knows everything about everybody in this town, including newcomers like yourself, and he's her right-hand man.

"Then why—?" Cat spluttered.

"Oh, I think it's obvious." Molly rolled her eyes.

"Not to me," Cat protested, longing to know.

"They think you're innocent," Molly declared matter-of-factly, "like the rest of us do. Hold still. I'll be right back."

She returned a few minutes later with a bouquet of the mountain laurel that grew wild in the woodlands. "Here." She thrust it into Cat's hands. Then she freshened up her hair, primping the curls laying against her temples and cheeks. "What do you think?"

Cat held the mountain laurels to her nose to give them an appreciative sniff. "All they need is a bit of ribbon."

"Coming right up!" Molly rummaged through the drawers of Cat's sewing cabinet and produced a wide silk ribbon Cat had been intending to use as a sash. "This should do." She returned to Cat to tie a cheery bow around the stems of the flowers. "They'll be easier to hold now." She handed them back.

"Thank you for everything." Cat cradled them lovingly. "I never would have made it through these last few days, weeks, or months without you. I wouldn't have even wanted to."

"That's what best friends are for." Molly's gaze misted with adoration.

Jack returned to the room to carry Cat to Jed's wagon.

We're getting married! Everything was happening so quickly that it was difficult to breathe. Jed and Molly must have felt the same way, because the four of them traveled in emotionally charged silence to the church.

Winifred Monroe followed behind them in her much fancier carriage. Rupert sat up front, holding his shoulders proudly.

As soon as Jed brought the horses to a halt in front of the church, Jack lifted Cat to the ground. She turned around and reached for her walking stick, but he reached for it first and handed it to Molly. "I'm more than capable of holding my bride up for our wedding."

She shyly smiled her thanks at him, thrilled to no end when he snaked an arm around her waist and walked slowly for her benefit.

Pastor Nathan Daniel was already standing behind the pulpit. "Welcome!" He jovially beckoned them forward.

Rupert rolled Winifred Monroe down the aisle behind them. "I'm here to witness the joyful event," she announced imperiously. "It's only right, seeing as how I've been serving as their chaperone."

"As well as my beloved employer." Cat twisted around in Jack's embrace to give her a warm smile.

Before she turned around, the door to the church opened and closed again, making her catch her breath. Billy

Bob had arrived, as promised. He moved farther into the building, striding down the aisle.

With a squeal of joy, Cat leaned away from Jack and fell into her brother's arms. "I am so glad you're here!"

"I wouldn't miss my own sister's wedding." He kissed her soundly on the forehead before depositing her back in Jack's arms.

He wasn't dressed up, but he was clean and wearing a freshly laundered shirt and black boots that were polished to a full gleam. Though he'd trimmed his hair, it still dragged his collar. To Cat, the best part about his appearance was the way his dark eyes glinted with pride and adoration. Never had he reminded her so much of their father.

She blinked rapidly, not wanting to weep through her wedding. "You look so much like Father," she choked.

The edge of his eyes crinkled at her. "I was about to say you look just like Mother."

"Thank you." Nothing else he could've said would've made her happier. She blew a kiss to him.

His expression grew mocking. "Are you sure about marrying a federal marshal?" He curled his upper lip at Jack. "It's not too late to back out if you're having second thoughts."

The way Jack's arm tightened protectively around her made her heart swell with joy. "I'm sure, Billy Bob. More sure than I've ever been about anything in my life. I love him so much."

He nodded matter-of-factly and raised his voice so that it would carry across the near-empty sanctuary. "I reckon there won't be a scalping today after all."

"Billy Bob!" Molly, who'd been standing nearby in silence, stepped to his side to swat his arm.

"I appreciate that." Jack's husky baritone rumbled through Cat as he tugged her closer still against his side. "You're so lovely," he murmured in her ear.

She blushed. "I'm glad you think so." Then she grew tongue-tied as she watched her brother reach for the hand Molly had swatted him with.

He continued holding it as he took a knee in front of her.

"Yes!" Molly gasped out the word before he could say anything. "I'll follow you to the ends of the earth, Billy Bob."

"As my wife?" He rasped out the question in a husky voice.

"Yes," she said again, smiling damply at him. "That would be a lot more respectable than the stowaway I was otherwise plotting to become."

He stood, chuckling, as he reached for her other hand. They stood on the other side of Cat and Jack, facing each other.

Jack nodded at Pastor Nathan, and he started speaking. "Dearly beloved, we are gathered here today in the sight of God and these witnesses to join together Billy Bob Flint and Molly Price in holy matrimony. We are also gathered to witness Deputy U.S. Marshal Jack Holiday and Catherine Rose Southerland being united in holy matrimony."

A commotion outside made everyone in the room tense.

Jack gestured for the minister to continue. "We'd better skip straight to the vows. I believe we're about to have a few uninvited guests." He sounded more resolute than surprised, which made Cat wonder what was really going on.

"As you wish." The minister glanced nervously toward

the door, before leading the two couples in front of him in a hasty set of vows.

"I do!" Molly and Billy Bob declared the words in joyous unison. Only seconds later, Cat and Jack uttered the same words while gazing deeply into each other's eyes.

Pastor Nathan closed his Bible. "Those whom God has joined together, let no man put asunder. I pronounce both couples to be man and wife in the name of our Lord Jesus Christ. You may seal the promises you've made to each other with a kiss."

Before they could do so, he ended the ceremony by speaking a rapid-fire blessing over them. Then he hastily had them and their witnesses sign their marriage certificates.

Jack exchanged a knowing nod with Billy Bob while he added his signature to his and Cat's marriage certificate, leaning closer to him so they could discuss in swift but careful detail what they would do after the Rangers arrived.

"Mark my words," Billy Bob intoned coolly, "the man behind today's shenanigans is none other than..." He uttered a name that drew a gasp from both Molly and Cat.

Without another word, Billy Bob claimed the lips of his bride.

JACK'S HEAD DESCENDED OVER CAT'S AT THE SAME time, deliberately blocking her view of her brother's silent exit from the back of the sanctuary. He was going to be alright. Molly was with him. More importantly, God would be with him, like He'd been from the beginning — all because Billy Bob had remained on the right side of the law.

The best thing Jack could do for his brother-in-law now was exactly what he was doing. His mouth moved tenderly over Cat's, promising he would love, cherish, defend, and protect her all the days of his life. It was no longer Billy Bob's job. It was his. The transfer had been made in the eyes of God and man.

When he raised his head to drink in her loveliness, she was glowing with so much happiness that it took his breath away.

A crash sounded in the back of the sanctuary as the door burst open and slammed against the wall. He turned with his new bride to face the swarm of uninvited guests. Six Texas Rangers parted ways, three flanking one side of the church and three flanking the other side. They converged on Jack and Cat with their weapons drawn.

"Where is he?" The first Ranger who'd entered the room gestured imperiously with his weapon.

"Who?" Though Jack was incensed over their brazen entrance into the church, he'd expected no less.

"Billy Bob Flint, of course!" The ranger looked flustered. "We were following the lead you gave us when we received a tip that he was headed back this way. One of the town's blacksmiths swore he saw him enter this very church not too long ago."

Calum MacIntyre. Billy Bob had been right about that detail, too, making the final piece of the puzzle fall into place for Jack. With how scarred Mr. and Mrs. Price were after the fire, it only made sense that they'd hired an accomplice — someone who'd been serving as their liaison between them and the townsfolk. Someone who could file reports about alleged crimes at the sheriff's office. Someone who could send and receive telegrams. Someone who'd known exactly who Molly and Jed Price were related to, making it that much easier to ingrain himself in their lives as a "trusted friend."

As far as Jack was concerned, everything was happening according to how he'd planned. Now that he knew who the real perpetrators were, it wouldn't take long to gather enough evidence to obtain three more arrest warrants.

"Another sighting, eh?" He forced a snarl to his lips as he faced the Rangers. "Search the church, just to be safe," he ordered harshly, knowing it would be best to take charge of the operation. "Every room. No one leaves the building without my permission."

Cat sucked in a breath. "Jack," she pleaded softly for his ears alone.

He bent his head to whisper in her ear. "Your brother is safe, sweetheart."

He raised his head and nodded grimly at Jed. "Secure the hitching post out front so he doesn't attempt to commandeer a horse."

"Yes, sir." Jed jogged down the aisle in the opposite direction of Billy Bob and Molly. The moment he was outside, he would lean around the building to give Molly the signal to drive away with the wagon of supplies they'd prepared for this very purpose. Billy Bob was carefully hidden beneath the burlap cover over the back of the wagon.

Jack continued barking out orders to keep the Rangers busy inside the building long enough for Molly and Billy Bob to clear the town limits. From there, it would be up to Billy Bob where he and Molly headed next. The fact that no one knew his ultimate destination would give Jack the plausible deniability that he needed to continue doing his job.

He managed to stall the Rangers the better part of an hour before he declared the outlaw was not on the premises. He shook his head at their small squad, regretting the necessity of sending them on yet another wild goose chase. It wasn't too long ago he'd suffered the same treatment at the hands of the woman he loved. "It must've been a false lead." He grimaced. "The only other sighting reported in the last few days was down near Dallas. I haven't been able to verify it yet, but it's possible he's heading south."

The Rangers exchanged various degrees of rueful expressions and opted to set their course for Dallas, leaving Jack to escort his lovely bride home in peace.

Winifred Monroe was kind enough to offer them a ride to the inn in her carriage. Before they disembarked, Cat gave her a tremulous smile. "Thank you for witnessing one of the most wonderful moments of my life."

Ms. Monroe's eyes glistened with emotion. "I wouldn't have missed it for the world." Then her voice grew tart. "Mind you, I'll need the proper amount of time to hire a replacement companion."

"I'm at your service, ma'am, until you do," Cat assured with a damp chuckle. "After that, I'll continue to visit often as a friend."

Ms. Monroe's expression brightened. "I'll be holding you to that, my dear!"

They said their goodbyes, and Jack proudly carried his injured bride into the Cedar Falls Inn to the room he'd reserved for a few more days. He planned to pay a visit to Sheriff Branch Snyder in the morning to discuss his job proposal in more detail. Afterward, he and Cat would start shopping for a home of their own, and he knew exactly which piece of land they would tour first.

"Welcome to our temporary home, Mrs. Holiday." He

deposited her on the chaise lounge and reached for a blanket to tuck under her sprained ankle.

Then he took a seat beside her to gather her in his arms. "I will do everything in my power to continue protecting Jed and Molly from the truth. The way Billy Bob pointed a finger at Calum MacIntyre today will help." He intended to make a big to-do over Calum's arrest to draw attention away from the two other arrests that would follow. There might come a time when it would make sense to tell Jed and Molly more. It was something he would pray long and hard about. In the meantime, Molly's marriage to Billy Bob had just finished ensuring that the very land her parents had stolen from his parents would now revert back to his name. Half of it would, at any rate. Cat's half remained in Jed's name for now, something Jack doubted she would object to now or ever.

Cat leaned closer, pinning him with a look of pure mischief. "You know more than what you're telling me," she accused in a teasing voice.

He adopted an innocent expression. "I can neither confirm nor deny that. It's against regulations for me to discuss an ongoing case with—"

His words grew muffled as she leaned closer to touch her mouth to his. "I know," she whispered against his lips, "and never have I felt safer than I do right now."

He knew it was her way of saying she was giving all of herself to him — her love and loyalty for life. It was deeply humbling to be the recipient of such devotion. More than he deserved. It was something he would strive to live up to.

He returned her kiss, anticipating the moment he would share his news about Billy Bob's wedding gift to them. Tucked beneath the very chaise lounge they were seated on was a chest loaded with coins. They'd been honestly earned from his many cattle sales. Inside the chest was a note encouraging them to use the money to purchase a few acres of rangeland adjacent to the Prices' farm that had once been lawfully theirs.

A whole new piece of land that will be lawfully ours!

Epilogue

One year later

Billy Bob held out a chair for Molly. She gratefully took a seat, gazing furtively around the near-empty dining room of the hole-in-the-wall inn where they'd rented a room the night before. They were circling through the heart of Texas right now, and he couldn't have been prouder of how well she'd handled the past year on the road with him. They'd ridden from one town to the next, never staying in place for more than a few days.

But as proud as he was, he was worried, too, more so than ever now that she was in the family way. The life they'd been living wasn't going to be sustainable for much longer. He'd been on his knees about it ever since his bride had informed him he was about to become a father. That was eight months ago. How the time had flown!

He reached for her hand as he took his seat, knowing he'd never get tired of gazing into her bluer-than-blue eyes and running his hands through her rich auburn hair. She was a gift from Above, his heaven on earth, his best friend, and perfect mate. However, that didn't mean it was right to keep her on the road with him. Not after the baby was born. They had some very big, very important decisions to make as she approached her due date.

"I know that look," Molly accused in a soft voice. She threaded her fingers through his. "You need to stop worrying about me."

"Can't," he muttered. His concern for her health and well-being consumed him these days. "It's not a fair request when you're two snaps away from giving birth to our son."

A joyful chuckle slid out of her that erased some of the tired smudges beneath her eyes. "You seem so sure about us having a boy."

"I am." He didn't know why. He just was.

"So cocky," she teased.

"So in love with you," he corrected, lifting her fingers to his lips.

They were fortunate she was such a skilled seamstress. It had been no trouble for her to alter a couple of her gowns to what she called an "empire waist." He couldn't have cared less what it was called. He was simply content to know she had clothing that fit comfortably. Today, she had on a gown the color of a sage plant with bits of crocheted ivory lace at her wrists and neckline. She was so beautiful, resourceful, and resilient that it made his heart swell.

"Worrying won't change a thing." She dropped his hand and reached for the menu. "Maybe the eggs and bacon here will be so delicious that it'll get your mind off of things."

"I don't want to get my mind off of things." He scooted his chair closer to hers to peer over her shoulder at the menu. Since their table was pushed against the wall, he trailed a hand along the underside of her swollen belly.

The baby kicked his hand none too gently, eliciting a gasp from her.

Billy Bob leaned closer to speak against her earlobe. "Are you still wondering why I'm convinced it's a boy?"

She gave another breathless chuckle. "Girls are strong, too."

"True." He couldn't argue with that. "Your strength never ceases to amaze me."

An elderly farmer approached their table, making him tense. In his experience, when folks came around uninvited, it usually wasn't a good thing. He kept protectively close to Molly while giving the man a warning look.

The farmer was unfazed by it. He nodded politely at them and held out a rolled-up newspaper. "I thought you might want to take a look at this, now that I'm done reading it."

"Thank you, sir." Billy Bob's shoulders relaxed. He half rose from his chair, eagerly accepting the unexpected gift. He and Molly were always hungry for news about the outside world. The way the wind was blowing politically in one area or another often influenced where they traveled next.

The older gentleman held on to the newspaper a second or two longer than necessary after Billy Bob's hand closed around it. "Page two is where you should start reading, son." After that cryptic statement, he walked away without looking back.

Billy Bob stared after him for a moment, trying to gauge if the fella was up to any mischief. However, all he did after leaving the building was untether his horse from the hitching post outside the front window. Then he rode away.

Just to be safe, Billy Bob waved their waitress closer.

"Who is he?" He nodded in the direction the farmer had taken.

Her expression lit. She didn't look much younger than the fellow who'd ridden away. "A very old friend." There was no denying the affection in her voice. "We grew up together and might've gotten married if my sweet Tom and his sweet Mary hadn't come along. Now we're both widowed, and he comes here for breakfast every morning. It's strange how life works sometimes, eh?"

"What a wonderful story!" Molly crinkled the edges of her eyes at the woman. "Thank you for sharing it."

"My pleasure." The woman eyed the menu Molly was holding. "What would you like for breakfast, ma'am? It looks like you're eating for two."

Molly gave Billy Bob an amused look. "My husband is convinced it's a boy, so I'd better order some bacon and sausage to go with my eggs."

"An excellent choice." The woman turned to Billy Bob. "And you, sir?"

Though Billy Bob heard the question, he didn't immediately answer. He couldn't. He was too stunned to speak. He'd opened the newspaper the older gentleman had given him and was poring over page two. What he was reading filled him with an indescribable emotion.

"Make mine a double order," he heard Molly say. "He'll have what I'm having."

"Coming right up," the waitress promised. "I'll bring some fresh milk and spring water to help you wash it down."

The moment she turned away from their table, Molly lightly flicked the newspaper Billy Bob was holding up between them. "What is it, love?"

Though he met her gaze, it took a moment for her beautiful image to come back into focus. "All the charges against me have been dropped." He couldn't believe it. It was everything they'd prayed for, but he hadn't fully believed it would ever happen.

She wordlessly reached for the newspaper.

He turned it around, pointing at the headline. It read, ***Robin Hood Vigilante Fights for Justice and Wins.*** The writer of the article had painted the name Billy Bob Flint into a glowing hero. He couldn't have been more astonished. He also couldn't have been more grateful for the part of the story she'd left out — the part concerning Molly and Jed's parents. There was no way it was an accident. He suspected his brother-in-law, Jack, might've had a hand in it. Only someone with connections could've pulled it off.

Molly scanned the first few lines of the article, reading the words beneath her breath about how Calum MacIntyre had been arrested. Apparently, he'd been traveling the panhandle for years, making false reports about Billy Bob to the authorities.

The last line of the article made her gasp. The author had written a heartfelt plea to anyone who read her article to help the authorities get the message to Mr. and Mrs. Flint that they were free to come out of hiding.

And that's exactly what one aging farmer with a newspaper in hand had done.

"Calum?" Though Molly looked ecstatic over their sudden change of fortune, disbelief warred with her joy. "I don't understand. Why in the world would a blacksmith trade such a good living for a life of crime?"

Billy Bob shook his head. "Maybe he found out a life of crime paid more than an honest living." Greed and the love of money made terrible bedfellows. A lot of folks welcomed them anyway, with little thought for how it would affect their eternity.

She nodded, growing tearful. "You know what this means, don't you?"

He knew what she was thinking, because it was the same thing he was thinking. A sense of profound relief filled him as he said the words aloud, "It means we can finally go home, darling."

"Home," she repeated in a trembly voice. Tears welled in her eyes. "Oh, Billy Bob! How I've longed for this day! And dreamed of it! And prayed for it!"

He let the newspaper fall to the table. Ignoring the few other patrons remaining in the room, he gently enfolded her in his embrace. "Yet you never complained about the way we've been forced to live. Never asked to change one thing about it." He couldn't have asked for a more loyal bride. Next to God, she was the most important part of his life.

She smiled through her tears at him. "Why would I complain when I have so much? The Lord. You. Our baby." She rested a hand on her swollen midsection. "Even so, I'm going to really enjoying letting my brother know he's about to be an uncle." She made a comical face. "He'll be every bit as cocky about it as you are about becoming a father."

"That he will." Billy Bob hoped they would be hearing some good news from Jed, as well, upon their return. "Maybe he's finally made some headway with the too-beautiful-and-elegant-for-her-own-good Bea Hazelwood at the Cedar Falls Inn. Perhaps they've even been courting in our absence."

Molly sniffed. "I sure hope not! Though Cat seems to like her, she and my brother will never suit." She sounded so matter-of-fact that he didn't press the matter further.

For him, it was enough that they were going home.

Home! Knowing Cat, she'd probably already purchased the land next door to Jed and Molly's property, which would make them neighbors. He couldn't wait to step foot again on the same patch of countryside he'd grown up on. To breathe in the good, clean breezes that swept across it. To round up a herd of cattle for him and Molly to tend to. To build a life together there.

Right after breakfast, they'd head to the telegraph office and send word to Cat and Jed — a message with three words only:

We're coming home.

The next morning

JACK SCANNED THE TELEGRAM THAT A COURIER HAD just dropped off at the sheriff's office. Waving it in the air, he shot out of his desk, giving a mighty war whoop.

Branch Snyder popped his head out of his office to see what was amiss. Catching sight of Jack doing a jig in the middle of the sheriff's department, he shook his head in bemusement. "For a second there, I thought Billy Bob or one of his range riders was riding through town." Real disappointment stained his features, though he tried to hide it with a grin.

More than ready to turn the man's grin into a real one, Jack moved across the room to wave the telegram beneath his nose. "He will be. Soon."

It had taken a lot of negotiating with his higher ups on both his part and the sheriff's part, but they'd ultimately agreed to make Jack's assignment in Cedar Falls a perma-nent one. His first case as the resident U.S. marshal there was to help the sheriff and his deputy round up the other set of cattle rustlers.

Though Jed and Molly's parents had been discreetly placed behind bars, alongside Calum MacIntyre, Longhorns and Mustangs were still disappearing here and there from the barnyards of the local ranchers. Sometimes one at a time. Sometimes two or three at a time. The perpetrators rarely targeted the same ranch twice, which was why it had taken so long for Jack to come to his latest conclusion — that there was another cattle rustling ring at work, one that had nothing to do with the operation the Prices has been running.

Fortunately, Jack and the sheriff had fine, upstanding citizens like Griff Jameson at Cedar Falls Inn serving as their eyes and ears around town. With the help of folks like Griff, they were confident they would shut down the other rustling ring soon.

Little did they know that more help was already on the way.

As the train rumbled down the tracks, Duke Stratton stood with a hand propped against the wall, gazing at the ever-changing landscape outside the windows of his train car. Like most bounty hunters, he didn't have the best reputation. Folks rarely had anything good to say about the gun-toting vigilantes who chased down the most dangerous hombres in the country — scoundrels with prices on their heads, and for good reason. They weren't exactly choir boys!

He'd made a fortune doing the government's dirty work for the past decade, but now he was ready to do something else with his life. He was headed to a remote cattle town out west to purchase a business, start a family, and settle into the role of a respectable gentleman. To speed things along, he'd contacted a mail-order bride agency and placed an order for the perfect partner to help him build a whole new life.

Mallory Price.

He silently rolled the name across his tongue, very much liking the name of the woman they were sending to him. It was classy and ladylike, and her story was equally fascinating — something about being the long-lost twin of a woman who lived in the very town he was moving to.

Though he'd never set foot in Cedar Falls, he was looking forward to helping his bride-to-be hunt down her long-lost sister. He was a professional finder of people who were lost or in hiding. Reuniting Mallory with a family member she'd been separated from at birth would make the perfect wedding gift.

Plus, it would make his new wife so grateful to him that she'd be more inclined to overlook his rougher edges.

Or so he hoped.

JACK SPED OUT OF THE SHERIFF'S OFFICE TO SADDLE HIS horse. Knowing Billy Bob's penchant for moving around the country like a ghost, anything was possible. He might already be within the town limits.

Branch Snyder followed him outside. "Don't leave me hanging, Marshal," he hollered.

Jack gave him a mock salute as he wheeled his horse around, silently promising to send word back after laying eyes on Billy Bob and Molly. As soon as he cleared Main Street, he gave Larkspur the rein to break into a gallop.

A rumble of thunder overhead made him cast a wary eye at the sky. Oddly enough, it felt like his initial arrival into town all over again...but in reverse. Fortunately, there was no stampede of Longhorns forcing him and Larkspur to seek shelter. Nor did any rain follow. It was thunder born of dry heat.

As he neared the homestead he and Cat had purchased, a cloud of dust arose, and a lone rider came into view. He was galloping in Jack's direction, but he slowed his horse as he approached.

Jack did the same. His heart pounded as he drew abreast of none other than Billy Bob Flint. He couldn't wait to send back word to the sheriff that the town's beloved local legend had indeed returned.

"You're home." Jack held out a hand, but Billy Bob ignored it.

He danced his horse closer to clap Jack into a bone-crushing embrace. "I couldn't have done it without you, brother."

Jack chuckled. "I had good reason. We're family."

Billy Bob let him go and sat back in his saddle. "It started before that. You rode into town with one purpose. Justice. And you got it."

Emotion tightened Jack's throat. He'd gotten so much more than that. A wife. A home. A family. A place to belong. He pointed beyond the cozy little farmhouse he and Cat were in the process of adding on to. "Are you ready to see it again?"

The old homestead Billy Bob and Cat had grown up on was barely a stone's throw down the road, and now he was going to get to live there with Molly. In preparation for their return, Jed had insisted on relocating to a smaller hunting cabin that was located on the property.

Billy Bob's eyes glowed. "I'm more grateful than you'll ever know." His voice was as hoarse as Jack's.

"Thank you for your wedding gift." Jack couldn't be happier about the prospect of living next door to Billy Bob and Molly. No doubt Cat was beside herself with joy, too. Ever since they'd purchased their farmhouse, Cat had made a habit of ending each day by the windows facing the Price farm, praying for Billy Bob's and Molly's safe return. She would be ecstatic to learn her prayers had been answered.

"You're more than welcome." Billy Bob snorted. "Believe me. There was no better wedding gift I could give my own wife than ensuring she and Cat would someday be neighbors."

Jack glanced around them. "Speaking of Molly, where is she?"

Billy Bob's eyebrows rose. "With my sister, of course." He angled his head toward the farmhouse.

"Well, what are we waiting for?" Jack eagerly pressed his heels to Larkspur's sides, urging her back into motion.

He and Billy Bob galloped the final stretch home and were greeted by the most stunning view in the world — the one every man would fight to the death for.

Cat and Molly were hugging on the front porch of his and Cat's home, and Molly looked close to bursting with child. He and Billy Bob couldn't leap off their horses and tether them fast enough to join their wives.

Cat's face was streaked with happy tears as she left Molly's arms and launched herself into Jack's eager embrace. "Thank you!" There was a world of joy and thanksgiving in her voice as she tipped her face up to his. Like her brother, she was convinced that it was her husband's intervention that had made her and Billy Bob's change in fortune possible. They had enough faith to know it was the Lord's handiwork, but they credited Jack for lending his heart and energy to the process.

Jack gave his wife a tender kiss, knowing the Lord had more than repaid him for his small part in the matter. Words felt inadequate, so he didn't try to come up with anything fancy. "I love you," he muttered huskily against her lips — right before claiming them again.

Minutes later, the four of them pressed closer to each other on the porch to gaze across the acres of farmland and pastureland that jointly belonged to them.

"Every inch of what we're looking at is lawfully ours." Billy Bob oozed with a brand of pride infused with the blood, sweat, and tears of a true frontiersman.

"Lawfully ours," Cat and Molly echoed, reaching for each other's hands without leaving the embrace of their husbands.

"Lawfully ours," Jack agreed. He would never get tired of saying those words. It felt as if his entire career as a federal lawman had been working its way up to this very moment.

And it was enough.

More than enough.

Thank you for reading
Lawfully Ours.

About Jovie

Jovie Grace is an Amazon bestselling author of sweet historical romance filled with cozy suspense and swoony cowboys. She also writes sweet contemporary romantic thrillers as Jo Grafford. To join her New Release Email List, visit www.JoGrafford.com.

For the most up-to-date printable list of her sweet historical books:
Click here
or go to:
https://www.jografford.com/joviegracebooks

For the most up-to-date printable list of her sweet contemporary books:
Click here
or go to:
https://www.JoGrafford.com/books

Happy reading!

Jovie

Made in the USA
Coppell, TX
27 April 2025